TALES FROM THE
SCAREMASTER™

ZOMBIE APOCALYPSE

You don't have to read the

TALES FROM THE
SCAREMASTER

books in order. But if you want to,
here's the right order:

Swamp Scarefest

Werewolf Weekend

Clone Camp!

Zombie Apocalypse

TALES FROM THE SCAREMASTER

™

ZOMBIE APOCALYPSE

by B. A. Frade
and Stacia Deutsch

Little, Brown and Company
New York Boston

Copyright © 2017 by Hachette Book Group, Inc.
Text written by Stacia Deutsch
Tales from the Scaremaster logo by David Coulson
TALES FROM THE SCAREMASTER and THESE SCARY STORIES WRITE THEMSELVES are trademarks of Hachette Book Group

Cover design by Christina Quintero. Cover illustration by Scott Brundage.
Cover copyright © 2017 by Hachette Book Group, Inc.

Little, Brown and Company
Hachette Book Group
1290 Avenue of the Americas, New York, NY 10104
Visit us at lb-kids.com

First Edition: April 2017

Little, Brown and Company is a division of Hachette Book Group, Inc. The Little, Brown name and logo are trademarks of Hachette Book Group, Inc.

ISBNs: 978-0-316-39894-7 (paperback), 978-0-316-39891-6 (ebook)

Printed in the United States of America

LSC-C

10 9 8 7 6 5 4 3 2 1

TALES FROM THE SCAREMASTER™

ZOMBIE APOCALYPSE

Don't make the same mistake
Ryan and Tyler made.
Don't read my book.

—The Scaremaster

I warned you.

Chapter One

"Tyler!" I called across the cramped and crowded costume shop to my brother. "You gotta see what I found!" I grabbed big boxes, small boxes, and thickly stuffed clear plastic envelopes in all sizes off the shelves until my arms were full.

A package of latex peeling skin got away from me and fell to the floor. There was no way I could pick it back up without dropping everything, so I left it where it landed.

"Where are you?" I shouted past frenzied shoppers looking for the best deals.

The costume shop was a small space. Tall display shelves formed mazelike aisles. Merchandise was so packed in that it made the already-tight store feel dark and mysterious. To me and Tyler that meant "extra-awesome"!

"Over here. In the makeup aisle." Tyler gave

what we called the "family whistle." One sharp burst followed by three softer tweets.

I listened closely to pinpoint the sound, then headed toward it, hurrying down the first empty aisle I found. I didn't want to waste time dodging shoppers. I was moving so fast my straight brown bangs flopped down over one of my brown eyes. Mom wanted me to cut my hair, but I refused. I could use the other eye just fine.

"Excuse me." A pale-faced, pencil-thin young woman with long black hair appeared in the center of the aisle.

"Whoa!" I didn't see her until it was almost too late. I managed to stop in time, but it was a serious near miss that could have been a big crash. I fumbled the things in my hands, and I dropped another package of fake skin. Oh well. I'd picked up so many of them, losing one more wouldn't matter.

"No running," she said, pinning me with her bright blue eyes. Her voice wasn't raised, like whenever I get caught dashing around school by the principal; it was calm and firm, kind of like Mom's when she gets angry. The woman scooped up the fallen package of fake skin but didn't offer it back to me.

"We don't act like monsters in *my* shop." She

handed me a plastic basket with two handles. "Put the items you wish to buy in here."

Heaving a sigh, I dumped everything I was carrying into the basket. I was in a hurry—couldn't she see that?

"Now can I go?" I asked, feeling impatient.

She held up a hand like a stop sign. "Let me see what you have."

The woman took her time going through the items I'd chosen. "Dirty, torn shorts, muddy, ripped T-shirts, red-colored contact lenses, artificial skin, bandages..." She neatly stacked it all, then handed the newly organized orange basket back to me, asking, "Zombie, right?"

"My brother and I are going to the school Halloween dance on Friday," I told her, feeling a surge of happiness. Halloween is my favorite holiday. "We're going to have the most amazing costumes!"

"I see." Her voice was now kind and soft. "You're certainly off to a good start." Her blue eyes seemed to shift to green when she told me, "You'll find your brother at the end of the next aisle to the left."

"How did you know—" I started to ask.

"Twins," she replied with a small smile that twinkled in her eyes, making them seem yellow.

"He looks exactly like you." She added, "Except for the hair." Tyler's was cropped short, the way Mom wanted.

"Of course," I said with a small nod. Being a twin was both a good thing and a bad thing. It was annoying when people mixed us up. But on Friday night, it was going to be epic when we mixed ourselves up on purpose.

"Go on," the woman said, pointing the way. "I'm sure you two have a lot of planning to do." She paused, still blocking my way and staring into my one uncovered eye for a few heartbeats before stepping aside so I could pass.

I shivered. There was a spark of something in the woman's now-brown eyes that made me nervous. She was nice enough, so I didn't know what was giving me the chills.

Using my "best manners" just like Mom would expect of me, I said, "Thank you, ma'am," and walked away.

Of course, my manners faded when I was out of her sight. With a quick look behind me to make sure she wasn't following, I took off running again.

"What took you so long, Ryan?" Tyler asked when I found him, exactly where the woman had said.

Suddenly, I felt as if someone was staring at my back, which was odd because I'd just checked. Now I double-checked. No one was there.

Shaking off the feeling, I held out the basket, jamming it toward Tyler. "I found some cool stuff."

My brother was a turtle. He took his time, slowly inspecting each item before asking, "Do we have to match?"

"Absolutely," I said, bouncing on my toes. We'd agreed a long time ago. "You promised me that we could be scary matching zombies when we went to middle school...and now it's middle school!"

"Oh." Tyler turned his attention back to the makeup. "I was sorta thinking we'd both be zombies, but you could be a crawler and I'd be a boney."

Boneys and crawlers were the most frightening kinds of zombies.

Tyler had spent a lot of time on the Internet reading about the undead over the past few months. He'd been the one to find this store. We had to take a bus, but the online comments said the man who owned it was an expert in monsters and would have everything we needed. The review was right about the costumes but possibly wrong about the man who owned it. I was pretty positive that the woman with the strange eyes was the owner. I didn't have any proof—she just acted like someone who didn't want me to mess up *her* store.

"Fine. Let's both be crawlers," I said. Tyler had told me that those were the kind of zombies with bad injuries that made them hobble along. They were really common in movies, and Tyler and I had seen a lot of horror movies. I hadn't known exactly what they were called until Tyler did his costume research.

I held up the shorts I'd found. "We can put fake blood all over our legs." I pointed at some tubes of blood on the shelf behind his shoulder.

"I really wanted to be a boney," Tyler countered. Boneys had their skin peeling off so that the bones showed through. He showed me these soft fake bones that you stuck to your skin to make it look like your bones were on the outside. There were leg bones and arms bones. They were kind of expensive, but I had to admit, they were really, really cool.

"Sure, great," I said. It didn't matter what kind of zombie we were, as long as we were the same kind.

For two and a half months, we'd kept our plans a secret. No one would be expecting what we were going to do. In fact, and just to really freak everyone out, Tyler was going to cut my hair short to match his right before the dance. We were going to shock everyone by appearing in two places at once! It was going to be a historic Halloween, one that would be remembered *forever*.

"Pick the makeup," I told Tyler. I really didn't care as long as it was scary. "I'll be whatever kind of zombie you want."

Tyler turned back to the makeup display. "Boneys," he said, more to himself than to me. "We need white and red and black...." He surveyed the selection. "Liquid latex, eyeliner, green slime, a lot of these fake bone pieces, and dark purple paint for bruises." All that went neatly into my basket.

I tried to be patient, but it was hard. Tyler wasn't just neatly organizing the things he found— he was organizing them alphabetically! When he finally took a pause, I snatched the heavy basket away before he could add anything else and fled to the register.

The woman with the changing eyes was at the counter. Without speaking, she nodded at each item as she rang up our choices. She didn't say a word until she told us the price.

7

Tyler looked at me with a horrified expression. "We don't have enough money."

"Are you sure?" I fished a combination of dollar bills and coins from my pocket. "We have all this!" I dumped our stash on the counter. It was every cent of our allowance and money we'd found in the couch since July. I'd even added two quarters I'd found on the sidewalk last week.

"I counted it last night," Tyler said, pinching his lips together while contemplating the glowing digits on the cash register display. "We're going to have to put a lot of stuff back."

I sighed as Tyler started separating the items into two piles. Most of the things I'd picked were ending up in the put-back pile.

"Can't we keep any of it?" I moaned.

"I don't think so." Tyler was distracted, adding totals in his head. "Makeup is the most important thing. Plus, it was my idea to come here...." he reminded me, as if that meant he got first dibs on what we bought.

"But—" I started to argue, when the woman at the counter cut in, saying, "I have a solution to your problem."

I'd honestly forgotten she was still standing there.

We looked up at her.

She crooked a finger. "Follow me." It was more of a command than a request.

Tyler glanced at me. We didn't just look alike; sometimes it was as if I could hear his thoughts. He wasn't scared, but he was more cautious than me. I knew he'd come along, but at his own pace after carefully considering her odd invitation. In the meantime, I wasn't waiting. I took off after her. Seriously, she owned the most amazing shop on the planet. What could go wrong?

I could feel Tyler's eyes burning into my back and knew he was scowling. But as I predicted, a second later I heard his footsteps behind me.

The woman led us through the store, down a narrow hallway, to the most incredible storage room I'd ever seen. The door was made of intricately carved heavy wood with a polished brass handle. It was awesome—perfectly spooky for a costume shop!

The hinges creaked as she twisted the knob and stepped inside.

"This is where I keep the discount items," she told us. "Only special customers get to come back here."

Leaning over to my brother, I said, "This is soooo cool."

It was like we'd won the costume shop lottery. The room was creepy. The woman was creepy. I couldn't wait to see what she had hidden here.

I pushed past Tyler and ran over to a shelf filled with items. There was a sign posted. "Seventy-five percent off," I exclaimed. "Check it, Ty!"

"That's a huge discount!" Tyler hurried over. We excitedly started searching through the items. "Forget what we picked outside. Everything we need is right here," he told me.

I expected the woman would leave us and go back out to her other customers, but instead, she moved to the side of the room and sat down in a chair that I hadn't noticed at first. This wasn't just a discount room. It was also her office, which confirmed to me that the online forums had been wrong. For sure, she *was* the owner.

The large throne chair, carved in a pattern similar to the door's, had interwoven circles and strange squiggled patterns along the back. It sat behind a clean, polished desk. The smooth surface reminded me of Tyler's desk at home. I hadn't seen the top of my desk in a long time.

I felt like we should hurry so she could go back into the busy shop, but the woman didn't appear to be in a rush. I looked at Tyler. He shrugged, and we silently agreed to take our time.

We started picking things off the discount shelf. Tyler organized what we wanted to buy into a neat pile, adding up the prices.

"You'll find expired fake blood, opened packages of peeling skin that were returned, and damaged bone pieces," the woman explained. "I can't sell any of it in the regular store."

"This is great!" Tyler cheered.

Then I noticed a box on the top shelf, just above our heads and a little out of reach. "What's in that?" I asked her.

"I'm glad you asked," she said with a small smile as she rose from the desk and stood on her tiptoes to bring the unmarked cardboard box down. She set the box on her desk. "You can have anything in here for free."

"Really?" Tyler checked. "Are you sure?" When she nodded, he stopped searching through the discount shelf, and we both went to look. "Free is even better than discounted," he said happily.

The things Tyler wanted were on the discount shelf, but everything I'd wanted was inside the free box! There were torn and dirtied costumes, similar to the ones he'd put back. It was amazing. There were slight package defects, but the box seemed to have two of everything I wanted: shorts, ripped T-shirts, packages of colored contact lenses, and long strips of loose bandages!

"Think we can have it all?" Tyler whispered to me.

I nodded. "She said 'anything.'"

I knew that he was wondering the same thing as me. Was it greedy to take the whole box?

Tyler decided to ask. "Can we—" he began.

The woman interrupted, answering even though he never finished the question. "It's all yours." She then took an old-fashioned ledger, a quill, and an inkwell out of the desk drawer and turned her attention to her work. I wondered again why she didn't go back out front to the store. What if other customers needed help or wanted to pay for their costumes? I hadn't seen any other employees.

It was strange, but she must have wanted to wait until we finished.

From underneath all the ragged clothing, Tyler pulled out an old book. He leaned in and whispered to me, "Hey, Ryan, check this out. Do you think she means we can have this book too?"

At Tyler's question, the woman raised her head and said, "The whole box is yours. I wouldn't have offered it if I didn't mean it." She noted the book in Tyler's hand. "It's a vintage journal. Practically an antique. It would be a shame not to use it." She stood, came across the room, and tapped the cover. "Perhaps you could draw your zombie costume designs inside." As quickly as she'd approached us, she went back to her desk.

"Let me see." I took the journal from Tyler. The book felt heavy and smelled like an odd combination of dirt and metal. I pushed back a little brass locking clasp on the cover and opened the pages. "It's damaged," I told Tyler. "There are these weird stains all over the first page."

"Maybe that's why she wants to give it to us for free," Tyler said. He took the book back. "It looks like marks from berries or grass." Holding the book against his chest, Tyler said, "I like it. We should take it."

On the bus home, I carried the free-stuff box. Tyler held the bag of discount makeup.

We were excited to go through our purchases. We didn't live far, but still, the ride felt like it was taking forever. To pass the time, I took the journal out of the box. I traced my finger over the strange triangle pattern etched into the cover. There were some long scratch marks dug into the leather, and I traced those as well.

"If only this book could tell us where it's been," I muttered to myself. Full of curiosity, I opened to the second page, the clean one after the berry-marked page, then made up a title and wrote it at the top.

"What else should I write?" I asked Tyler.

"I don't—" Tyler started, when suddenly, I jumped up, grabbing Tyler's hand and squeezing it hard.

"No way! What the heck?!" I gasped.

The bus driver told me to sit back down.

"What is going on?" Tyler yanked back his hand.

Without another word, I lowered myself into my seat and turned the book toward my brother. I'd written:

Awesome Zombie Costumes

Under that, mysterious handwriting had appeared:

Zombies, is it? Oh, the Scaremaster knows a thing or two about the undead. You shouldn't have started this story. Now I get to finish it!

Chapter Two

We'd tried to get the book to "talk" to us again on the bus, but it didn't work. No matter what I wrote, the pages stayed the same with my title and the Scaremaster's spooky response.

When we got home, all we wanted to do was keep on exploring whatever it was that happened on the bus, but as fate would have it, Mom was waiting. And she'd brought pizza.

I swear my legs were shaking so hard under the dining table that it looked like I was having a seizure, while Tyler downed three slices of pepperoni in less than a minute.

"Tomorrow's Monday, and I've got homework," he told Mom, tossing his plate in the sink and making a dash toward the stairs.

"Me too!" I said, though that was probably the most suspicious thing ever to come out of my mouth. I couldn't think of a time that I had ever hurried off to do homework.

Ever since Dad left and moved away, dinner has been a sacred time for us as a family. A huge wave of guilt swept over me as I glanced back from the stairs to see Mom sitting alone at the table with her half-eaten slice of pepperoni.

I shoved the guilt aside.

Tyler was waiting.

Tyler and I shared a bedroom. His half, like his desk, was neat. Mine wasn't. To prevent fights, Mom hung a curtain down the middle of the room, dividing the space so Tyler didn't have to look at my mess and so my mess didn't creep over to his space. It worked, mostly.

I was half a second behind Tyler. When I got upstairs, he was already on his perfectly made bed, holding the mysterious book.

"What took you so long?" he asked.

"I—"

He interrupted. "Kidding."

I jumped onto his bed next to him, and we stared at the journal.

"Should I open it?" Tyler asked. There was a tension in the air. We didn't know what we'd find inside.

Some people might have thought the book was scary, but not us. Tyler and I weren't afraid of anything. We'd seen so many horror movies that nothing fazed us.

We laughed at blood and guts. Big bugs, man-eating aliens, ghosts…bring them on! We never jumped at the bad-guy-popping-up parts. Seeing the actors scream with fear was hysterical.

Sometimes, on the weekend, we'd have a marathon and watch three different movies in a row. My favorite ones were action films with big monsters and high-stakes chase scenes. My least favorite films were about vampires, with slow-moving suspense and mystery plots. Tyler was the opposite, so together, we watched them all.

The more we tried to scare ourselves, the sillier it seemed.

Finding this old journal felt like we were in a movie.…We were still at the beginning, right after the opening credits, where anything was possible.

"I'm so excited." Tyler ran his hand over the strange design on the journal's cover, tracing the triangles with his finger, like I'd done on the bus.

He was taking too long, so I snagged the book. "Hey!"

"Tyler the Turtle," I said, using the nickname Mom gave him when we were little.

"Ryan the Rabbit," he replied, knowing I hated being called that. But then again, being a rabbit, I hopped into action and twisted the latch. The cover fell open. "What the—" I exclaimed.

The pages were all blank. Even the berry stains seemed to have disappeared. I looked through the whole book. Nothing was written anywhere.

I turned to Tyler. "Ah, man. Did I imagine what happened on the bus?"

Tyler shrugged. "Weird. Even though we share matching chromosomes, it's highly unlikely that we imagined the exact same thing." My logic-loving brother took the book back from me and flipped through the pages himself. The book still smelled like dirt and metal, but otherwise, it was just a plain journal.

"Well, that's that, I guess," I said with a long sigh. "I'd hoped it was really possessed." As if that were possible...Nothing in horror movies ever really happened. But it would be cool if it did!

"We should have known it was a gag book." Tyler took the journal again and flipped it over. "How does it work? Disappearing ink? Maybe there's a computer attached?"

"We didn't have Wi-Fi on the bus," I reminded him. While Tyler mulled that over, trying to figure out how the book had talked to us, I came to a realization. "Who cares how it works? It's spooky looking, and that still makes it cool. I say let's get started on those awesome costume ideas. We only have five days till the dance."

I took a pencil from the cup on Ty's desk. On the first page of the book, I drew a stick figure with shorts and a T-shirt, then asked Ty, "Where do you want to put the bone pieces we got?" I pointed to the ankles. "Here? Or higher, like on the shins?"

"I think—" His words weren't even fully formed when writing appeared under my drawing.

Want to hear a story?

My artwork faded away.

Across the top, the page now said in a deep cursive scrawl:

Tales from the Scaremaster

"Whoa!" Tyler grabbed the journal back from me. "Awesome! We gotta find out how it works before the ink disappears again." He started chopping at the cover with a pair of scissors. "This must be the best grade of leather ever," he said, showing me that his art scissors were now bent, but that the cover wasn't marked. "I'm getting a kitchen knife." He headed to the door.

"Wait, Ty," I stopped him. "Who would spend their time and money planning a prank against two kids they don't even know?"

Tyler came back into the room. "Maybe we are on one of those joke TV shows?"

That seemed unlikely unless there were cameras in our room, in which case Mom would be in on it, which was even more unlikely. She didn't have much of a sense of humor. "Or…" I said in slow breathy voice, "maybe, fingers crossed, the book's really haunted after all?"

"That would be neat…" Tyler said, quickly

adding, "though about as likely as your TV show idea."

I knew supernatural possession was a long shot, but there was only one way to find out.

"Let's write in it," I suggested. "If it's obviously fake, then you can stab it with a knife."

Tyler agreed.

The Scaremaster had asked if we wanted to hear a story, so I wrote:

Yes.

The tale started right away:

Once upon a time, there were twin boys, one named Tyler and the other, Ryan.

Okay, so that was strange, but in a positive way. I raised the pencil to write:

How do you know our names?

The story continued without answering the question.

They believed they weren't afraid of anything, but the Scaremaster knows everyone is afraid of something. The Scaremaster would reveal their greatest fears.

"What's he talking about?" Tyler looked at me with a puzzled expression, then back at the book, where more handwriting appeared.

On Monday morning, frights will begin. Which twin will be the first to admit he's truly scared?

I looked at Tyler, and he shrugged. "What's he gonna do to me?" Tyler wondered. "Write a spooky story about a twin who finds sticky trash on his desk and a knocked-over pencil cup?" He wrapped his arms around himself. "Ooooohhhh," he said in a mocking voice.

It was true. That was probably Tyler's biggest fear, and it wasn't very scary. For me, we considered ways I might get scared, but came up blank. Not even a spooky book that talked back frightened me. In fact, I thought it was great. What were the chances it really *was* possessed by a disembodied soul? Ha. Real frights... How cool would that be?

We're in, I dared him. **Do your scariest.**

The Scaremaster seemed to accept the challenge and wrote:

> *There was a girl named* _____
> *who was afraid of spiders.*
> *The very thought of them gave*
> *her the chills. She couldn't go*
> *camping and mostly stayed*
> *inside, just in case a spider might*
> *crawl by.*

"I guess he's taking his time getting to know us while he figures out our fears." Tyler raised his eyes from the page. "This story sounds a lot like he's talking about Maya," he said.

When we were in kindergarten, Mrs. Walterson

read us a book about the adventures of Sally Spider and her friend Gordy Grasshopper. Maya began to cry so hard she had to go to the nurse.

I thought Maya had grown out of it, until last year when we went on a field trip to the science museum. She refused to get off the bus when she heard there were spiders on display inside, even though they were dead and pinned to viewing boards. Her dad came and picked her up.

Out of curiosity, I filled in the blank where her name would go.

Maya

The Scaremaster changed my handwriting to match his own, then went on using Maya's name in his tale.

When he was done, I tried writing back.

If you want to scare us, why write a story about Maya?

There was no answer.

Chapter Three

The screaming was so loud I could hear it all the way across the lunchroom.

"Is that Maya?" Tyler asked me, his mouth full of hamburger.

"Nah." I brushed off the possibility, then reconsidered. "We'd better check."

We left our lunch trays on the table and followed the shrieking.

It *was* Maya!

There was a crowd of teachers around her, so it was hard to see what had happened, but her friend Rachel was holding court by the wall, sort of like a press conference for the curious. Rachel reported that when Maya had opened her lunch box, hundreds of spiders crawled out onto the table. They scuttled onto Maya's arms and legs, even getting in her hair.

I squeezed through the crowd to get a look, and

sure enough, a gaggle of fuzzy black spiders was scurrying across the floor. There were so many they looked like a flat black cloud as they moved together.

Both students and adults were hurrying out of the spiders' path.

"Eww," I heard someone say.

"That's a health code violation for sure," I heard someone else mutter.

One stray spider had lost the pack and was crawling near Tyler's foot. I pointed.

"Unsanitary," he moaned, making me realize who'd declared the health code violation. "Should I step on it?"

Whenever there were bugs in a movie, stepping on one created more. It was as if they were primed to multiply. I said this to Tyler, and he agreed.

"Seems prudent to be cautious," he said, kicking it across the room with the side of his shoe instead. We watched as the lone spider immediately joined its brothers, who were now crawling up the wall.

Without even looking at Tyler, I knew we were both wondering whether this had anything to do with the Scaremaster's story.

Maya's terrorized screaming had ended, and the room was silent except for the school nurse, who was pushing his way through the students.

The mass of spiders had formed a thick black line and was escaping out an open window. With the exception of a couple of kids who really loved bugs, everyone was keeping their distance. I would have liked to go check the spiders out but decided sticking near Maya was more important. Tyler and I had a few questions we needed answers to.

"What happened?" the nurse asked Rachel, who had unofficially become the source of all information.

"She screamed, and then she fainted." Rachel was short and skinny, wore glasses, and had long blond hair pulled up into two pigtails. I was pretty sure that, like me and Ty, Rachel wasn't afraid of anything.

Nurse Dixon was more concerned with whether or not Maya had hit her head on the bench than where the spiders came from, though he did want to catch one to make sure they weren't poisonous.

"They aren't poisonous," I told Tyler, a bit too loudly.

"How do you know?" Nurse Dixon turned to

me. He'd been a military nurse in an active war zone, which made him a hero—and intimidating.

I'd never lie to Nurse Dixon, but what was I supposed to say?

The Scaremaster's story talked about scaring Maya, not killing her. Then again, there was still the possibility that this didn't have anything to do with the book. It could just have been a random infestation.

"Uh, I saw them," I said after an awkward pause. "They didn't look dangerous."

"Still," Nurse Dixon said, "I'd like to see one for myself." He called over Mrs. Clancy, who was the school's head janitor.

She took her job very seriously, saying, "I'll get a spider for you, then call the exterminator." Mrs. Clancy added in a deep and compassionate voice, "I hope the young lady is all right. Arachnophobia can be a terrible thing...."

A few minutes later, Maya had recovered from fainting and was able to walk out by herself. As she left the cafeteria, her glazed-over brown eyes settled on my face.

"What?" I mouthed.

She didn't say anything but also didn't look

away, staring at me until I finally blinked and dropped my eyes to the floor.

"I have the book," Tyler told me when we went back to our lunch trays. He reached into his backpack and put the Scaremaster's journal on the table between us.

"I think we should hide that until we get home," I said, recalling the look Maya gave me as she was escorted out of the lunchroom. Her shoulder-length brown hair was tangled and sticking up at odd angles. Her clothes looked wrinkled, like she'd been pulling at them, trying to get the spiders off her. But it was the look that would haunt me for hours. She was terrified—that was certain—but there was a message in her eyes: Maya thought I'd been the one to put spiders in her lunch box!

I hadn't done it! I really liked Maya. I'd known her longer than anyone else at school, except Tyler, of course. Her family came from Korea, and every time she went to visit her grandparents, she brought back the best chocolates. They were so yummy, and I'd never do anything to her to stop the candy flow.

That's what I told Tyler.

"I know you didn't put spiders in her lunch box," he told me.

Which led me to say, "And I know you didn't either." Though I reconsidered and asked, "Did you?"

"Of course not!" Tyler was insulted, as if him doing something so evil was even a possibility. "There were only three people who knew about last night's spider story in the journal. So if it wasn't us, that leaves the Scaremaster." He put one hand on the journal. "Now can we cut this apart and see how it works?" Tyler was always so logical. In the last few minutes since Maya had left, my own theory had solidified.

"It's possessed," I said firmly. I had to admit, the conclusion thrilled me. "We might be the only people on the planet with a truly supernatural, possibly demonic book. How cool is that?!"

"If only..." Tyler replied with a grunt. "Unfortunately, like how behind every great movie is a special-effects person making the scares look scarier, I know there's an explanation to the book. We just have to discover what's behind the pages."

"No, Ty, I'm serious. It's almost Halloween, and the lady at the costume shop gave us a possessed book!" I said it loudly so there could be no doubt I was serious.

Tyler shushed me so other kids wouldn't hear. "No way. We've seen every movie, heard every 'true life' horror story, read a zillion possession stories—and as much as we want them to be true, we always find some logical flaw." That was true. "Someone else knew about Maya's spider fear." He stood. "I'm going to ask Cook for a knife. She probably won't give me one, but I'm still going to ask. If I can get one, we can slice through the cover and the binding and find out how it works. Scissors bend too easily."

While Tyler went to the kitchen, I opened the journal cover.

Under the Maya spider story was a new question:

That was scary, right?

I dug through my backpack for a pen.

I had to admit I still liked the idea of frights before Halloween. Just not that one. It was scary to Maya, but it was way too mean. The Scaremaster, who or whatever he was, wanted to play games, so let's play. I wrote: **No. Not scary.**

Well, then let's try a
different story.

There was a boy named _____
who was afraid of dogs. He was
walking home from school when
a dog broke through a fence and
began to chase him.

I knew who he meant. There was only one kid at school that was so scared of dogs he would get all freaky and weird if one barked, even if the dog was miles away.

It felt good to have it figured out, like on the rare occasion that I knew an answer on a pop quiz. Without considering what might happen, I filled in the blank with the name **Eddie**.

Again, my handwriting morphed into the Scaremaster's and the story continued.

Eddie ran, but the dog was
faster. The twins tried to
help him escape, but he was

wild with fear. He ran into a neighbor's yard, where he fell into a swimming pool. The twins couldn't help but laugh, seeing Eddie, wearing his school clothes and backpack, floating in the pool.

I was frowning when Ryan came back to the table. "As I predicted: Cook won't give me a sharp knife. She said for 'safety' reasons students couldn't have knives." He made air quotes around "safety" as if that was the dumbest thing he'd ever heard. "I can handle a knife," he grumped, settling back in at the table to eat the last bites of his hamburger.

I didn't respond. I silently turned the book toward him. "Read this."

Tyler was quiet for a while, then asked, "Is this all?" He turned to the next page to see if there was more. There wasn't.

The last words the Scaremaster wrote were:

Maybe that will be scary enough for you.

Chapter Four

The next day, I heard the dog bark before I ever saw it.

Eddie never screamed. Some people, when they are scared, can't muster even a squeak. I hadn't known that about Eddie, but when Tyler and I ran toward the dog's vicious growls, we immediately realized he was one of those people.

Eddie was standing on a pathway between two houses. This was the shortcut we all took into our neighborhood. Eddie lived on the street behind our house.

He must have left school before us, because my brother, turtle toes, wanted to drop off a book at the library. Where normal kids might drop and dash, not Tyler. He couldn't leave one without checking out a new one, and picking took time.

By the time we got into the alley, the dog, nearly

the size of a small horse, was facing Eddie, who was frozen like a statue in the park.

The beast was black with sharp teeth and matted fur that looked like it had never been brushed. It was growling, drool dripping from decayed gray gums and wolflike fangs. I'd never seen this dog before in the neighborhood.

"Eddie," I said, coming into the alleyway, "don't move." Of course, instead of hearing "don't," Eddie must have only heard "move," because he started to run backward, toward me and Tyler.

The entire Scaremaster's story then came true, even the part about me and Tyler laughing at the end, though we tried desperately to hold back.

Eddie saw that he was trapped between me and Tyler at one end of the alley and the ferocious beast at the other. The dog bared its teeth, and although Tyler and I would have moved aside to let Eddie run past, Eddie's brain wasn't processing options very well.

I'd seen this same situation in the movies a thousand times but never in reality.

Eddie couldn't make good choices, so he made a bad one. In a fit of fear and panic, he scrambled up and over the nearest fence. It was a six-foot chain-link barrier around a backyard that housed a pool.

The beast leapt after him without hesitation. It dragged itself over the fence in such a carefree way, it seemed to be part dog-beast, part giant monkey.

Behind the monster, Tyler and I followed. My shoelace got caught up in the fence, and Tyler had to pull me over. I guess Mom was right that I should keep my shoes tied. She's so smart sometimes....

As we landed on the other side of the fence, Tyler shouted to Eddie, "Stop. Wait. Come back this way."

If Eddie moved toward us, instead of moving farther into the neighbor's yard, we could create a distraction and lure the dog away from him. Tyler and I weren't scared of dogs, not even this giant one, so we'd have an advantage.

Eddie was way past terrified. His logical brain had shut down. He saw the pool and—without considering whether the dog could swim, or that he was wearing his school clothes, or without really thinking at all—jumped in.

He landed with a splash.

Turned out that was a pretty good choice after all. The massive mutt didn't follow. In fact, it bared its teeth one last time, as if to say, "I dare you to EVER shortcut through my alley again," then turned, hopped easily back over the chain-link fence, and disappeared down the path.

That was when we laughed.

Later that night, when the Scaremaster asked whether *that* prank was scary, I didn't answer right away. It was endlessly terrifying to Eddie. But to me and Tyler, scary wasn't the right word: "Bizarre" was better. It was bizarre that the stories written in the book seemed to be coming true. Not just that, it was bizarre that Tyler and I were being blamed.

It didn't matter that we knew we weren't behind Maya's spiders; Rachel had started telling everyone about that wild look Maya gave me and how I'd announced they weren't poisonous (which they weren't). Those facts led to a rumor that I'd been the one who put the spiders in Maya's lunch box. Since Tyler and I did everything together, the rumors sucked Tyler in as my accomplice. Just like that, we were guilty without evidence or trial.

Eddie's doggy nightmare was certain to make it all worse.

I didn't think that Eddie would ever talk to us again. When he crawled, dripping wet, out of the pool, his backpack and all his schoolwork ruined, Tyler and I stopped laughing and looked at each other. He was so mad, his whole face was red-hot.

Eddie had dropped his phone when he jumped the fence. I found it and gave it back to him before we all went home, but the look in his eyes pretty much told me we were not going to be friends ever again.

We were getting ready for bed when I decided to answer the Scaremaster's question. He'd written:

The dog chase scared you, right?

Me? No. It scared Eddie. Not me.

I was feeling angry about who this was and why he or she or it was doing these pranks, so I wrote:

No!!!!!!

I added a whole lot of extra exclamation points for emphasis, and then I shut the book.

Tyler came into the room with an arsenal of kitchen weaponry in a cardboard box. There were several knives, a meat cleaver, a cheese grater, and a potato peeler. Mom had taught us both to cook, so we knew how to use kitchen tools properly. What Tyler planned wasn't at all proper. Mom would be upset if she found out.

"Special circumstances," Tyler said, setting down the box. "Since Cook wouldn't let me use hers at school, I have no choice but to use Mom's." He raised her sharpest blade over the journal's cover, like he was about to commit bookicide— that would be a fancy way to say "book murder." "First we find out how this thing works. Then we find out who's behind it," he said.

I still believed in my possessed-book theory, but it felt better thinking that there was a person behind the pranks so we could stop him (or her).

Tyler slammed the knife into the front cover with a mighty *"hi-ya!"*

"Uh-oh," I said as he stepped back from the book. Mom's favorite knife was bent at the tip. "Hammer it flat," I suggested. "She'll never know."

Tyler frowned. "That'll never work."

Mom was smart, and we both knew she'd be mad. But Tyler didn't seem overly worried. He was determined, no matter what, to get into that book cover.

After he had bent two more knives and broken the potato peeler off its handle, I told him to set down the meat cleaver. "We have to leave her something to cook with," I said, adding, "or we'll starve."

He looked at the book, then at the broken weapons. "What kind of book is this? Why can't we open it? We'll never know how it works!"

I gave him a long knowing look, to which he replied, "You're wrong, Ryan."

I shrugged. We were back to my original, and now only, conceivable theory. "Supernatural possession," I said in a soft voice.

Tyler shook his head. "I'm going to find out who's behind this and what they want." He opened the book and wrote:

Who are you?

The Scaremaster

What do you want?

A scary Halloween

Are you a person?

I'm the Scaremaster.

"See?" I told Tyler enthusiastically. "Not human." Tyler tried again: *What are you?*

The Scaremaster

"This could go on all night," I told Tyler. "How do we get him to stop?"

"I guess we ask nicely," Tyler said, reminding me of the good manners Mom always talked about.

I agreed to try. I loved a good prank, but what had happened to Maya and Eddie wasn't funny.

Tyler raised his pen to ask the Scaremaster politely to stop terrorizing our friends but froze when a new story appeared.

There was a girl named _____
who was afraid of clowns.
Thanks to Ryan and Tyler,

*tonight would be the scariest
night of her whole life.*

"He's going after Soon-Yi," Tyler said, a mortified look on his face.

I was the only one on planet Earth who knew about Tyler's crush. It started the first day of school this year when Soon-Yi sat next to him in math and asked what page they were on. He hadn't actually talked to her since, but that didn't keep Tyler from always knowing what page they were on, just in case she asked again.

Knowing that her name went on the blank story line, I grabbed a pen to write it in.

"Wait!" Tyler stopped my hand. "I'm not sure the Scaremaster can identify who in our class has which fear. We keep adding the names to the blank line. It's like we're telling him who to terrorize."

"So what do you want to do?" I asked. There were times that Tyler's slow consideration of a problem was good. This was one of those times. I'd have already written poor Soon-Yi's name and let the clowns attack. Instead, Tyler took his time, reflecting on the situation until he had a plan.

"Let's put in someone else's name," he suggested. "Someone who isn't afraid of clowns."

"Write my name," I said, handing him the pen. "Clowns are dumb."

Tyler hesitated. "The Scaremaster, *whatever* he is, is pretty smart. I think he might know there are no other Ryans in our class. And certainly no girls named that."

I thought about the girls at school. It would be too complicated to text anyone and ask if they were afraid of clowns. What was I going to say? "Don't panic, but...how 'bout Mom?" I suggested. "She's not afraid of anything."

"She's not in our class," Tyler replied, though I could see he was thinking about it.

"Hear me out," I said, getting into the idea. "She's a nurse. She sees blood all the time. She sees gross wounds and hears real-life scary stories all day," I told him. "I bet she can handle a few psycho clowns."

It took a few more minutes, but I convinced Tyler it was a good idea. I felt satisfied that whatever the Scaremaster had planned for tonight would fail as I wrote Lucy into the blank spot for the story.

As it had happened every other time, my hand-writing disappeared and he re-wrote it in his own cursive scrawl.

"Oh no!" Tyler exclaimed as the Scaremaster changed the name to his own handwriting and started the story fresh.

The story wasn't about "Lucy" as we expected, but rather the Scaremaster had written "Soon-Yi."

Tyler looked at me with bulging eyes and said softly, "I have a bad feeling...."

I bit my bottom lip. "Me too."

Chapter Five

Wednesday morning, Soon-Yi wasn't at school.

And worse than that, no one would talk to us.

"What are we going to do?" I asked Tyler over chicken nuggets and tater tots. It was my favorite lunchroom meal, but I couldn't enjoy it.

The way things were going, we'd have no friends by the dance on Friday night. If we didn't have friends, who'd care if we switched places? No one. Our big Halloween scare was going to be ruined! While I liked hanging with Tyler, I couldn't imagine talking to only him—for the rest of our middle school career.

I was beginning to despise the Scaremaster.

I decided to tell him that.

"Hand over the book," I said to Tyler.

He gave me a blank look.

"Don't pretend you don't have it," I said. "I know you brought it to school."

"I was going to see if Mrs. Clancy had a blow-torch or battle-ax in the janitor's office," Tyler said. "Well, maybe not a battle-ax," he corrected himself. "But a weapon bigger than a kitchen knife. We gotta break this book open."

Having a possessed book was not nearly as fun as I had thought it would be. Even if Tyler didn't agree it was possessed, we'd come to the same conclusion: It was time to get rid of the thing.

Sure, we could have just ditched it in the field behind school, but then someone else might find it and the scary stories might keep on appearing. Plus, it felt wrong to carelessly toss out the Scaremaster's journal. I worried that the Scaremaster would be really mad if we did, and who knew what might happen to our friends then?

On the subject of what to do with the book, I was now 100 percent with Tyler. We needed to destroy the Scaremaster's journal forever.

"Can I see it?" I pushed my tater tots around on the plate with a fork.

"Oh, fine, but don't get the Scaremaster started on another story. We have to put an end to this!" Tyler set the book on the table. There was no evidence on the cover that he'd ever even attempted to damage it. The book was looking newer and newer every day. I sighed.

"So if Mrs. Clancy won't lend us a blowtorch, what other book-destruction ideas do you have in mind?" I asked, but before Tyler could answer, the Scaremaster wrote:

Did you hear about Soon-Yi?

I showed the question to Tyler, who turned red with anger. "I told you not to start anything!" He snagged my pen out of my hand.

Tyler wrote:

She's not at school.

She may never come to school again.

WHAT DID YOU DO?

Tyler was furious. There were no Soon-Yi rumors yet, so we hadn't heard what happened. Rachel must have been behind on the news.

I told Tyler to call Soon-Yi, but he said he couldn't.

"I haven't talked to her since that first day, so it would be weird to start now," he explained.

"But we're concerned," I said, feeling the hair rise on my neck. "Maybe you can pretend she's sick and offer to deliver her homework after school."

"I can't." Tyler shook his head. When it came to his crush on Soon-Yi, he was super shy. He could barely talk to her at school, there was no way he could go over there and have a whole conversation at her house. I nearly laughed because it seemed like my brother was more afraid of Soon-Yi than of the Scaremaster.

There was only one way then to find out what had happened to her. We needed the Scaremaster to tell us the rest of the Soon-Yi story, but when we asked, the Scaremaster simply wrote: *The end.*

Then that disappeared, and a new story began.

Without reading it, Tyler crossed out the Scaremaster's words as fast as they appeared. When there was a small pause between paragraphs, Tyler wrote in the blank space:

No more stories!

The Scaremaster immediately replied.

I'm not finished.

Whatever he'd been writing dissolved, and the page suddenly looked clean, white and new. I had an eerie shiver as writing appeared:

Three days till Halloween and the big party at school. So much scaring left to do.

I felt like I could hear him laughing at us through the book.

There were a lot more kids in our class, some probably didn't have big fears, but I was certain there were other kids who had hidden phobias.

"Let's say there are ten kids without any fears." Tyler was using his math skills to work out the probability. "That leaves about ten more who have them, give or take a few. Three days till the dance, so on average, he has to scare three and a third kids per day to get them all." Tyler wondered, "What awful stories could he tell?"

My brother and I knew a lot about fears. That came with our obsession for scary stories and movies. Every time we'd watched a frightening film, we looked up the phobias that the movie was about. It was amazing how many things there were that scared people.

"I know who has achluophobia." I pinched my lips together. "In science, when we were doing a unit on electricity, Mohammad told me that he is scared of the dark." I wondered if the next story might be about him.

"How about astraphobia, fear of lightning and thunder?" Tyler said. "Someone might have that."

"Poor Eddie already faced cynophobia," I said. That meant fear of dogs. "How about ophidio-phobia?"

Tyler shrugged. "Snakes give a lot of people the creeps." He tacked on, "Not us, of course, but other people."

"Shhh…" I put a finger to my lips. Tyler was talking too loudly. I hoped he hadn't just given the Scaremaster a snake-scare idea! But so far, the author seemed to respond only to writing in the book. I didn't think he could actually hear us through the pages.

I happened to glance down at the book, which was still open on the table.

A new story had begun. This one was actually titled "Acrophobia."

I couldn't remember what that meant. I had to ask Tyler.

"Heights," he said with a long sigh. I knew he was upset that another story was starting. "When does this end?" he muttered.

We both fell silent, thinking about everyone we knew, trying to discover who was going to be the star of this story.

I didn't have any idea who in our class might be afraid of heights, but there was a niggling feeling in the back of my brain. I'd heard of someone... but who was it?

The Scaremaster then began.

Once upon a time, there were twin boys, one named Tyler and the other, Ryan.

If I never heard someone say "Once upon a time" ever again, I'd be happy.

The Scaremaster was the master at scaring, but now it was their turn.

I whipped around to look at Tyler. "What does he mean by that?"

Tyler was still so mad about whatever had happened to Soon-Yi, he quickly wrote in thick, heavy print:

We have our own scary plans for Friday night. Back off!

I raised my hand for a high five. "Way to tell the Scare-monster who's boss!" We slapped palms. That didn't stop the story.

The twins threw Mr. Ramirez's car keys onto the roof of the school.

"Oh, darn," I told my brother. "Now I remember who's afraid of heights. Remember the carnival at the start of the school year? Mr. Ramirez refused to climb the rock wall." Tyler and I went, like, fifty times each. The view from the top was amazing.

"Not Mr. Ramirez!" Tyler gasped. That was almost worse than Soon-Yi. We'd started Spanish classes this year, and he was our favorite teacher.

On test days, he always brought a piñata, and anyone who finished his or her test got to take a swing. Last week, Tyler was the one who broke it open. There were prizes and candy inside. Even though I didn't do very well, it was the best test ever!

I wrote in the book:

We aren't throwing his keys on the roof. He's afraid of heights. Plus, he's a teacher. You can't play pranks on teachers.

That's what makes it scary!

Not happening.

*I've done all the scares so far—
don't you think you should take
a turn?*

I wish I had thought to take a photo of that last line. It was the proof that we weren't behind all the scary stuff and maybe, just maybe, our friends would understand that this creepy book was doing it all. Actually, I wished I'd been taking video all along! If we had film of the spiders or the dog, everyone would know it wasn't us pulling the pranks.

Of course, I didn't think of it, and now the writing was quickly fading. Plus, none of that was possible anyway, since phones weren't allowed in school. The Scaremaster probably knew the rules and was laughing at us.

Tyler took the pen and tried to reason with the Scaremaster.

No more stories. We don't like them.

Are you scared yet?

No. Just annoyed.

*I suppose we need more
stories, then.*

We still hadn't tried asking the Scaremaster politely to stop writing stories. I told Tyler to give it a go. He wrote:

When will this stop?

When you are scared.

I looked to Tyler and said, "That will never happen."

After thinking about it, Tyler decided to write: **Okay. You win. We're super scared. Please stop.** Tyler even added: **I might cry.**

I laughed. That was absurd. Then again, why not tell him we were frightened? If scaring us was what he wanted, we could let him think he'd won.

The Scaremaster wrote back: *I don't think so. I'm not done here yet. You will be scared soon, though. Count on it.*

It was my turn to write. Obviously, Mom's good manners didn't apply to supernatural demon-possessed books and their paranormal authors.

I wrote in big letters: **ENOUGH!**

The Scaremaster replied in one word.

No.

There was more writing that showed up in broad paragraphs, but we agreed that we didn't want to read the story. If we didn't know what was supposed to happen, maybe it wouldn't. And if something bad did happen, then we could say we didn't know anything about it, right?

Tyler slammed the cover shut. I locked the clasp.

We put the book into Tyler's book bag and choked down the last cold bites of our lunch.

"Has anyone seen my keys?" That was how Mr. Ramirez began class.

Tyler sat at the desk next to me in the crowded classroom. He didn't look at me but kicked my ankle instead. I kicked him back but missed.

"*¿Dónde están mis llaves?*" he tried again in Spanish. No one replied. Mr. Ramirez was tall and thin, and, according to Rachel, rumored to have been a semipro basketball player in Mexico before moving here to teach. I didn't know if that was true, but he *did* coach the school team.

A small, scared voice came from the side of the room, near the exit. "Can we help you look for them?" It was Maya. She'd been at school all day, but she looked really pale and sat so close to the door in every class that I imagined she planned to run away at the slightest sign of a spider.

Kids from around the room chimed in, in Spanish, with easily formed questions like "When did you see them?" and "Where were you at lunch?"

He told us they had to be in the classroom and he really needed them; otherwise he wouldn't interrupt class like this. He had an important meeting off campus next period.

We all got up to look around. That's how much everyone loved Mr. Ramirez.

Tyler met me in the back of the room by the supply closet. "What do we do?" he whispered.

"He'll never think to look on the roof," I said, wishing there was a way for me to secretly go get the keys.

Tyler raised crossed fingers. "Maybe they aren't there?"

I snorted. Of course the keys were on the roof. We both knew it, and we both knew who put them there.

After five minutes of looking, Mr. Ramirez finally told us all to go back to our desks. He'd start class and search again later. "I was so sure they were in my jacket pocket," he muttered in English. He checked his coat one more time.

"*Bueno,*" he said, moving on. In Spanish, he said, "Let's review homework."

Tyler raised his hand. He didn't even give Mr. Ramirez time to call on him before blurting out, "I know where your keys are."

Uh, as far as I was concerned, that was *no bueno.* First, Tyler was about to get in big trouble, and second, he wasn't talking in Spanish. So that meant even more trouble.

I whispered, "What are you doing?"

He leaned over to me and whispered back, "This is *my* moment. I know it is. The Scaremaster was right about revealing my biggest fear!"

I looked at him out of the corner of my eye. "What are you talking about?"

Tyler sighed. "I'm afraid of getting in trouble." He gave me a small smile, since "trouble" was my middle name. "No offense."

"None taken." Duh. I should have known. I've known him my whole life! How did I miss this?

Even when we were toddlers, when I threw my cereal on the floor, he ate every bite of his. When I knocked over a tower of blocks, he rebuilt it. Once

I finger-painted on the wall, and instead of joining the fun, he got paper towels to clean it up.

In school, he always refused to trade places with me, which I always wanted to do.

All of the time I have spent in detention, I have spent alone.

Agreeing to trade places at the dance had been an easy choice for him. It was Halloween. Scary things were expected. There'd be no "trouble" for what we'd planned.

Oh, Tyler...

I looked at his face and knew he wasn't kidding around. His eyes were wide and his jaw hung loose. His breathing was fast and shallow. The guy was so pale he was practically see-through.

I seriously thought he might faint like Maya did when she found the spiders.

"You know where my keys are?" Mr. Ramirez asked to be clear he'd heard correctly.

Tyler swallowed hard and nodded.

It was like a brick hit me in the head. I realized in a flash that the Scaremaster's new story wasn't actually about Mr. Ramirez or the keys. It was a trick, meant to scare Tyler. The Scaremaster had done what he said he'd do. He dragged out Tyler's one and only fear and revealed it to our classmates.

What was really frustrating was that the Scaremaster caught on before me.

I simply said, "I wish I'd known...." All along, Tyler had been scared of getting in trouble. There was probably a phobia name for it, but I didn't know it.

Tyler took a deep breath and stood up. There was a spark of bravery beneath that fear. "I am going to beat the Scaremaster by facing my fear," Tyler whispered to me as he passed by. "We have to change the story." He nodded at me with a look that confirmed he no longer thought the book was a human invention. He'd come around to my belief that it was something otherworldly.

I wondered how much Tyler was going to explain to our teacher. Did he know how to say "possessed journal" in Spanish?

I made a spontaneous decision. If Tyler was going down, I was going with him. Of course, I wasn't scared, so I had nothing to lose.

I stood up and announced in English, "The keys are on the school roof."

The Scaremaster had asked if *we* were scared. We tried lying, but that didn't work, so this was our way of shouting "NO." Standing together, *we* weren't scared of his stories and *we* weren't scared of getting in trouble either.

Mr. Ramirez called us both to his desk. Softly, so other kids couldn't hear, though I knew Rachel was straining to listen with her eagle ears, he asked, "How do you know where my keys are?"

Tyler asked permission to go to his backpack. He brought out the journal.

We walked by Rachel on the way back to the front of the room. The look on her face was unreadable. She stared at the book in Tyler's hand, then passed a glance from me to Tyler and back again, like we were at a Ping-Pong match. After that, she inhaled sharply. Then she moved forward, leaning at an awkward angle over her desk.

I knew she was listening when Tyler told Mr. Ramirez, "This book tells stories that come true."

I glanced back at Rachel. Her expression still revealed nothing. Could she hear us?

I was certain she would spread whatever rumors she wanted, and I couldn't stop that, so I put my back to her as Tyler opened the cover's clasp.

I was uncomfortable about showing our teacher the book, especially with Rachel leaning so far toward us that she was going to get a neck cramp. But he seemed genuinely interested, and if any teacher could help us figure out how to make the stories stop, it was Mr. Ramirez.

Tyler opened the book. The first page was blank. My stomach fell. The story about his keys should have been there.

"When we write in it, the Scaremaster answers back," Tyler said, for the first time admitting out loud there was something more to the author than a prank. And to prove it he wrote:

Tell us a story.

Nothing.

We want to hear a scary story.

Nothing.

Mr. Ramirez frowned. "Sorry, guys," he said. "This smells like a pretty big Halloween prank. I heard about Maya, Eddie, and Soon-Yi." His eyes darted from me to Tyler. "Are my keys really on the roof?"

I nodded.

Tyler wasn't ready to give up on the book yet and was now scribbling **Where are you?**

"All right." Mr. Ramirez gave Tyler a cool, steady stare. "No more fooling around. Put the book away." He told the class to work on the next page in our workbook, then told us, "Come on. Let's go." He stomped into the hall, clearly furious. We quietly followed.

I could tell that Tyler was a wreck inside. His eyes were dragging the floor, and his breathing was out of control. He was truly scared.

I whispered, "Detention isn't so bad. It's a nice quiet time to catch up on homework." Which was good since I was always behind. Of course, that wasn't helpful to Tyler, so I added, "You could get ahead, or start learning advanced calculus, or take up another language." I showed him how to hold his head high and stare down anyone who might be looking at us.

He glanced at me, clearly unconvinced that detention was a positive thing.

At first, Mr. Ramirez headed toward the principal's office, but then suddenly he paused. He stopped so fast that I nearly ran into his back. "We're going the wrong way," he told us in a strange, flat voice.

Huh?

"Come along," Mr. Ramirez said, rotating one hundred eighty degrees on his heel. "We need to go in this direction."

To our surprise, he led us away from our punishment, down the hall to a small janitor's closet, where there was a long ladder attached to the wall.

In another surprise, the closet door was unlocked. It was never unlocked; believe me, I checked all the time.

"You two stay here," Mr. Ramirez told us. He started up that ladder only to stop partway. He came back down. His face was ghostly white, and his hands were shaking. "I can't do it," he admitted, putting his head into his hands.

"Fear of heights?" Tyler asked, though we already knew it was true.

He nodded. "I got stuck on a roller coaster when I was a kid. Ever since then, I've avoided high places."

"I'm not afraid," I told him. "I'll go." I stepped up onto the first rung.

Just then a woman's deep voice resonated through the small closet. "I heard there was a problem." Mrs. Clancy popped her head into the room. She shooed us all aside. "If those keys are on the roof, I'll get them."

Three minutes later, I found out what happened at the end of the Scaremaster's story.

Mrs. Clancy fell off the roof. She dropped thirty feet onto the school bushes with a crash. When she landed, her leg was bent at an awkward angle.

"It's our fault," Tyler said. His voice was filled with regret. "I wish she hadn't gotten hurt. I wish I knew how to end this before someone else has to go to the hospital."

"I wish that stuff too," I told him.

As far as anyone knew, we'd been the ones to set this disaster in motion. We threw the keys, we took the blame, we were at the ladder when Mrs. Clancy climbed it, and we were on the lawn watching her scoot down the slanted roof toward the keys when she fell.

"What's the longest you've ever had detention?" Tyler asked me, though I was pretty sure he knew the answer.

"A few days," I said, thinking this time we might be in for it until we graduated middle school.

Seeing our janitor all crumpled up in a bush, with her coworkers tending to her, was heartbreaking.

Again, not scary but very cruel. We felt bad for whatever our role had been, even if the real villain here was the Scaremaster.

"The Scaremaster wanted to scare me by getting me in trouble," Tyler reasoned while the ambulance sirens approached in the distance.

"Are you scared?" I asked. Maybe if the Scaremaster got what he wanted, this story-game could end here and now.

"No," Tyler said. "I'll never be afraid of getting in trouble again. It's better to face what I've done and take the punishment." He paused. "I think tonight I'll tell Mom I broke her kitchen knives, grater, and potato peeler." At least for now, Mom thought they were just missing.

I was really proud of my brother. Tyler wasn't going to let the Scaremaster scare him anymore, even if it meant detention at school *and* being grounded at home.

"So what happens next?" I asked him.

Tyler gave me a pathetic look. "You positive you don't know what scares you most?"

I shook my head.

"Well, then we can't prepare for it," Tyler said. "We can't break the book apart. We can't ditch it around here. So there's just one option: Together, we are going to have to face whatever is coming."

I wasn't sure I liked that option, since I was the target, but the lesson here was, when the Scaremaster tried to frighten me—and he would—I needed to stand up to it, like Tyler had done. Head-on. That was the only way to change the story. But what if I did that and the Scaremaster pivoted, just like he'd done today—injuring someone else in the process?

I didn't know what to do!

Mrs. Clancy was lying on a stretcher when she called me and Tyler to her side. She looked petrified and stared at us with unblinking eyes. Her hands trembled when she gave me Mr. Ramirez's car keys.

"I have barophobia," Mrs. Clancy said, her fearful face scrunched up in a grimace as she fought against the pain in her broken leg.

I had no idea what that one was, so I looked to Tyler. As the paramedics rolled the stretcher into the back of the ambulance, he sighed. "Fear of gravity...as in falling."

The Scaremaster had ended another story.

Chapter Six

When Tyler's alarm went off, we should have started getting ready for school, but neither of us really wanted to go.

It wasn't because of detention. Our punishment wouldn't start till Monday, since the faculty was all too busy planning the school dance to stay after and supervise us for the next two days.

It wasn't because of the dance either. We'd gotten lucky with that too. Even after Tyler showed Mom the damaged knives, avoiding an explanation of how it had happened, she still said we could go. And the principal agreed.

Neither of us wanted to go to school because of the Scaremaster. I was solidly convinced that he was behind the delayed detention and had somehow manipulated things for us to go to the Halloween dance. He wanted us there. But why?

Before bed, we'd opened the book to check for

a new story that might give us a hint of what to expect, but the pages were blank.

Tyler hit snooze, and I cuddled deeper into my covers, stalling.

"Are you afraid of what might happen today?" Tyler asked me.

"Afraid?" I echoed, my voice muffled by the blankets. "No. I'm not scared, but I don't want to walk into a trap either."

"I've been thinking...we need to find out more about this book," Tyler told me. "The dance is tomorrow. Who knows what the storyteller has in mind between now and then?"

I was about to ask him what he thought we could do, but Mom popped her head into our room. "You guys aren't up yet? What's going on? You'll be late."

I heard Tyler mutter softly, "Just add it to the list of things we're already in trouble for...."

I started to laugh but didn't want Mom to think we were joking around. I choked on the giggle, and the laugh morphed into a moan. I didn't mean for it to be so loud, but Mom took it as if I was moaning because I was sick.

She pulled back the curtain between our beds and rushed over to me. She put her hand on my head. "I don't think you have a fever."

I sat up, saying, "I'm fine."

If we were sick, that could be the thing that would make us miss the dance. There was no way I was missing it, even if no one but Tyler talked to me all night. Even if the Scaremaster did his worst to frighten me. I was going to dress like a boney zombie and dance until my feet fell off!

I dragged myself up. "Come on, Ty, we gotta get ready for school." I started running around, looking on the floor for something clean to wear.

"I have an idea. How about you two stay home and rest today?" Mom looked at me, then Tyler. "I want you two healthy for Halloween."

I got the sudden chills.

Oh, Scaremaster, what were you up to? There was no way that in a normal world Mom would *want* us to stay home sick from school and still go to a party tomorrow.

If Tyler had any remaining doubts that the

Scaremaster was supernatural, this latest weirdness should prove it.

Mom left the room, then came right back. "I have to work today, but Dr. Rasmussen left these new multivitamins for the staff to try. They aren't for sale yet. It's a special blend he invented. He said they 'cure everything.'" She laughed. "Obviously that's not true, but they'll probably help with whatever you two are coming down with."

She handed us the vitamins and gave us each a kiss on the head, saying, "I'll be back around three." She pointed at the vitamin in Tyler's hand. "Take it." Then to me, "And rest."

Mom scooted out the door, and a few minutes later, we heard the garage door close.

I leapt out of bed and put the vitamin in my desk drawer. We didn't need them. We were healthy and fine. Tyler put his in a drawer too.

Since we couldn't destroy the book, Tyler had decided we needed a way to get rid of it. Something where there was no risk of another kid at school finding it and the Scaremaster continuing the stories.

Ty took out the book and set it on his desk. The cover fell open.

"Did you—" I started to ask.

"Must have been the wind," he said, though the windows were closed and the ceiling fan off. He peered down at the first page. "Here's the story we've been expecting," he groaned. "Let's find out your fear, Ry."

But it wasn't a story. The writing said:

Good morning! Think of all the scary things that could happen today. I can barely contain my excitement.

"I think he's threatening you," Tyler told me.

"I know," I said, feeling powerless.

"Hmmm." Tyler paused. I was getting a headache from his active brain. Sometimes this twin power is a pain, literally. He was silent for a long time, then jumped up and blurted out, "Since we don't have to go to school, let's go back to the costume shop."

"Genius, Ty! Let's visit the woman with the weird eyes," I said. "See what she knows about the book, since she was the one who gave it to us!"

"I didn't know you noticed her eyes!" Tyler's voice rose in an excited way. He quickly found his shoes and slipped them on without untying the laces. "We're going to give her back the book."

An hour later, the bus dropped us off near the costume shop.

We burst through the door to discover the shop was packed with customers. It looked like everyone in town had taken the day off to do some last-minute shopping.

We wove our way through the crowd to the checkout counter. An older man was standing behind the register. He had gray-brown hair and wire-rimmed glasses. He was wearing a vampire cape and false teeth.

We had to wait in line.

When it was our turn, Tyler plopped the old journal down on the counter.

"Howww caaan I help yooou?" the man asked, rolling out the vowels to sound like Dracula.

"We need to return this," Tyler told him.

The man peeked over his glasses. "I've never seen this book before." He dropped his accent.

"You got it here?" With a long manicured finger, he traced the etchings on the cover.

"Yes," Tyler and I said at the same time. Then Tyler added, "We don't want it anymore."

The man took out his teeth. He drooled a little and wiped his chin with his sleeve. "Do you have a receipt?"

"No," Tyler said. "It was free. We just want to give it back to the woman who owns the store."

"I own the store," he said, looking extremely puzzled.

The line behind us was growing, and people were getting antsy. A large woman with three hyper kids was tapping her foot.

I had to ignore her and concentrate on the conversation.

"Do you have another clerk?" Tyler said. "She took us to the back room and let us see some sale items."

"And a box of free stuff," I chimed in, pointing again at the journal.

"Long dark hair. Color-shifting eyes." Tyler added, "She told us that the journal was one of a kind."

"There's no one working here fitting that description. And there's no discount area. Are you sure you kids are in the right store?" the man asked. He glanced over us to the line that now snaked down the aisle.

Tyler nodded. "One hundred percent."

The man picked up his fake teeth and turned them around in his hand. "I can't take that back because I didn't give it to you." Looking down at the book, he told us, "If it was free, why not give it away or throw it out?"

"We can't—" I started, but Tyler cut me off before I could explain how this supernatural book was writing evil stories and how we didn't think throwing it away would stop its tales.

"Do you have a trash can?" Tyler asked.

"There's a dumpster out back." The owner tipped his head toward the room where the woman had taken us, but added, "You'll need to go around the building."

"Sure," Tyler said. He swept the Scaremaster's journal off the counter and headed toward the main door.

The woman behind us muttered, "It's about time...let someone else get to the register."

I snarled at her.

The man at the counter put in his teeth. "Howwww caaan I help yooou?" he asked her in his Dracula voice.

Tyler started toward the front of the shop but then ducked around a corner. "You give up too easily," he said, showing me his new "face trouble" attitude. He stepped in front of me. "Come on."

The store was so crowded that it was easy to blend in. We moved step by step through the people to the back of the shop. The area we'd been in, where the offices were, now had a big, worn-out Employees Only sign posted.

"We came all this way only to be told that there's no mysterious woman. No free stuff. And the guy at the counter looks like the guy described in the online reviews." Tyler boldly marched past the sign, head high like I'd taught him. "Something is fishy. Let's investigate."

A minute later, we were standing in front of a normal door that led to a normal storage room with a normal desk and shelves packed with brand-new stock.

"This is so odd," I breathed. I kept expecting something to pop out. Maybe there was a fake door panel that led to an alternate storage room?

But before Tyler and I could discuss it, a teen-aged boy wearing an astronaut costume nabbed us by the shoulders. "What are you doing back here?" he asked, his breath sounded heavy, like a real astronaut in space.

I had a reply ready. "We got lost on the way to the dressing room."

I was a bad actor, but Tyler was worse. "It's not back here?" he asked, glancing around the room pretending that he'd just realized this wasn't the dressing area.

"Where are your costumes?" The astronaut was smarter than us. Our hands were empty, except for the book Tyler held.

"Did I say dressing room? I meant bathroom," I said, grabbing my belly and crossing my legs like a four-year-old.

"Up front." The astronaut didn't let go of our shoulders. He pushed us toward the main part of the store. I crossed my feet and let myself trip, bumping hard into Tyler, intentionally knocking the book out of his hands.

It slid across the floor, stopping underneath that plain-looking desk.

Tyler went to grab it, but I hissed, "Leave it.

That thing belongs here. We can honestly say we returned it to its owner."

"Let's go, boys," the astronaut said, tugging us along.

Tyler took one last glance at where the book was now partially hidden by the desk's shadow. He nodded at me and then said, "We were just leaving anyway."

Chapter Seven

Mom's car was turning onto our street just as we were getting off at our bus stop around the corner.

"Run!" Tyler shouted.

We bolted behind a house and cut through the park, getting home and inside mere seconds before the garage door opened.

We leapt up the stairs two at a time and were both in our beds, under our covers, when Mom called up, "Boys, I'm home."

We were wearing our clothes, sweaty, flushed, and breathing heavily, when Mom came in.

"You guys look awful," she said. "I brought more of those vitamins. Dr. Rasmussen really thinks they'll help get you back on your feet for tomorrow." She came to my side first and handed me two vitamins. "He advised me to up the dose." Mom handed the pink capsules to me and gave me a kiss on my head before doing the same for Tyler. I knew the "kiss on the head" trick was to check our temperature but didn't let on.

She wore her long hair in a tight bun for work. After removing the pins, she stood at the end of the curtain so she could talk to us both at the same time. She said, "I'm not sure how well the vitamins will work, but I'll make chicken soup for dinner. Every mom knows that's what *really* cures everything!" She laughed at her own joke, then kept on giggling as she made her way down the hall.

I let out a huge breath. "Too close," I said, opening my drawer to put the vitamins inside.

"Augh!" I jumped back so fast that I accidentally got tangled in the curtain between our beds. It fell to the floor with a whoosh.

"What?!" Tyler came to my side so quickly I thought he should join the track team.

I pointed.

The Scaremaster's book was in the drawer.

"No way!" I said, reaching out to take it.

"Don't touch it." Tyler stopped me. "This confirms that he's after you now." He looked me over from top to bottom. "Are you scared yet?"

"Is there such a thing as bookaphobia?" I snorted. "It surprised me, that's all. But no more than the popping-up parts in a movie. Are *you* scared?" I asked. Not that it really mattered, but I was curious.

Tyler considered the question. "Honestly, no," he said.

Comparing our reality to horror films, this was how the story was meant to go. The Scaremaster was directing a classic movie plot. Just when the main characters thought they were safe...*dah, dah, dah*...they weren't.

I took the book and plopped down on the floor, right were we were standing. I opened the cover, and as expected, there was a new story. "We gotta read it."

Once upon a time...

I really, really hated that beginning.

...there was a boy named Ryan.

Yep, Tyler had been cut out.

He pretended nothing scared him. He told everyone he had

no fears. But the Scaremaster
knew the truth.

Tomorrow night, at the dance,
Ryan would know real fear.

His plan to scare the others
would haunt him.

One zombie, two zombies, three
zombies . . . zombies everywhere.

"Are you afraid of zombies?" Tyler asked me.

"No." I said, considering the Scaremaster's words. There was no way the entire school was going to show up as zombies. As Tyler would say, statistically speaking, it was improbable.

"I'm gonna force the Scaremaster to leave us alone," I said firmly, as if that were possible. I crossed the room to get a pen out of Tyler's cup and was about to write something strongly worded when I noticed something odd. There were crumbs in the page creases and chocolate chip smears on the page edges.

"Were you eating cookies the last time you opened the book?" I asked my brother.

"No. What?" It was as if he didn't hear my question. He was thinking. "If I'm afraid of getting in trouble, what are you afraid of? What does the Scaremaster think he knows?"

"I don't have a clue...." I said truthfully, sweeping the crumbs out and onto the floor.

"Really? No ideas?" Tyler asked. "Whatever is in that book comes true. We can't destroy it. And we can't get rid of it." He shook with a whole-body shiver. "Doesn't that scare you? Even a little?"

I shook my head.

"If a supernatural book doesn't scare you," he asked me, "what does?"

I didn't have an answer. Was it possible that the Scaremaster knew more about me than I knew about myself?

Friday at school crept by slowly. No one talked to us. If Wednesday afternoon was bad, taking time off had made things worse for us both. Rachel had had a whole day to build on the anxiety that Tyler and I were going to find out everyone's greatest fears and scare them. No one wanted to be next, so everyone stayed far away. Even the teachers ignored us.

"I can't wait for school to end," I told Tyler when we met for lunch.

After school, we'd get dressed for the dance, then, after dinner, come back to school.

"Let's work on our makeup ideas." Tyler had brought the journal with us, figuring that if we left it at home, it would show up in his backpack anyway.

We had it, but that didn't mean we had to open it! Instead, I took a blank sheet of notebook paper from my own backpack. I drew a circle head and said, "Don't forget we have to cut my hair this afternoon."

Tyler's eyes gleamed. He didn't seem worried about getting in trouble anymore. He just wanted to have fun at the dance. In fact, he had some crazy ideas of times when we could trade places and double the scares.

This was going to be awesome. I drew marks across the face to show where scars could go. Tyler liked the one by the eye but not by the lips, so I erased that one and added peeling skin there instead. We shaded under the eyes and added blistering skin on one cheek.

"Cool," he said. "Draw a body, and let's decide where the bone pieces can go."

"Put that sharp bone closer to the knee," a voice behind us said.

It was so shocking that anyone was talking to us that we both leapt back. I almost knocked over Tyler's milk. The person behind us reached forward and nabbed it just in time. Spill avoided.

I looked up. "Soon-Yi?"

"Are you surprised to see me?" she asked. I could tell she was teasing. "I came to say thank you." She set down Tyler's milk.

Tyler's jaw dropped so far open it practically rested on the table. I shoved his leg with my foot. He looked at me. "Talk," I mouthed.

"Uh...you're welcome...why?" he asked. I thought that was pretty good for his second time speaking to her.

Soon-Yi was a dancer. She was thin and always wore dance clothes since she went straight to dance class after school and never had enough time to change. Her nearly black hair matched her eyes. Those eyes were now staring at Tyler as she spoke.

"I know you were behind the scary clown that popped up in my window the other night."

Tyler didn't speak, but he shook his head.

"It's okay," she said, setting a hand on his shoulder. "Rachel told me how you two have been scaring everyone all week."

Tyler shook his head even more adamantly and managed to say, "Not us."

"You don't have to pretend," she said. "I'm not getting you in trouble." She smiled as if she was in on his big "scared of getting in trouble" secret.

"Your spooky clown appeared in my bedroom window, on my computer screen, and on my phone screen. Later, there was a projected clown car image above the bed with an endless number of clowns piling out." She closed her eyes. "That one was the worst."

I was surprised by how many images the Scaremaster had managed. She must have been terrified.

"I didn't sleep all night." As she said that, she laughed. "I stayed home because everywhere I looked, I thought I saw clowns. My mind was playing scary tricks on me." She shook her head as if to get rid of the memory. "But then Rachel told me what you did in Spanish class, Tyler," Soon-Yi said.

He blushed but clearly didn't understand.

"When you told Mr. Ramirez that you'd

thrown the keys on the roof and faced getting in trouble for that...it was the right thing to do. Rachel told me that you were really brave and honest. That was when I realized I also had to face my fears to overcome them!" She gave us a big smile and said, "I'm going to dress like a clown for the dance." Taking the pencil from me, she flipped my page over and drew out her own makeup. "Big red lips, puffy nose, blue around my eyes..."

When her sketch was done, Tyler said, "Wow." Then, to my huge surprise, he blurted out, "Can we dance together?"

Ha! In that moment, I knew he'd faced another of his fears. I hadn't even known that Tyler had one fear, but now it was clear he had two. His inability to talk to a girl he liked was a small, sort of silly fear, but still, seeing him overcome it was awesome!

"Of course!" she said happily.

Things really were looking up. Tyler's inspiration was contagious. Soon-Yi told us that Maya was going to be a spider and Eddie had found the perfect dog costume.

"I thought the Scaremaster's story said everyone

was going to be a zombie!" I exclaimed after she walked away. "He's so wrong!"

Tyler grinned and said, "Once again, the story's changing." Then his eyes brightened. "Hurry," he said. "We've got something important to do."

"What?" I asked.

"Soon-Yi gave me an amazing idea." He smiled at me as we approached a table of eighth graders. "We probably can't scare the Scaremaster, but we can beat him at his own game. The Scaremaster's days of scaring are about to end."

Chapter Eight

When Tyler and I arrived at the dance, we were certain we had the Scaremaster beat. We were the only zombies, so already he was wrong. And as for scaring people based on their fears, we'd solved the problem. If the Scaremaster couldn't scare me, he wouldn't be able to scare anyone else, as he'd shown with Tyler.

When Ty had faced his fear, the Scaremaster had moved on, knocking Mrs. Clancy off the roof since she was afraid of falling.

Now, if he didn't scare me, there was no one left to scare. We were one step closer to beating him at his own storytelling game.

As for us, we weren't feeling motivated anymore to scare people. We agreed we had had enough of that, and even though we looked awesome and had the same haircut so we looked alike, we decided to be silly instead of scary.

Tyler and I were wearing everything from the costume shop. We'd had a discussion about whether or not the clothing and stuff might be possessed too, since the lady who gave us the book also gave us the box, but in the end, we decided we were being paranoid.

We put on the dirt-covered shorts and tattered shirts. Then we dug into the makeup. The fake blood was a little funky, since it was expired. It dried really fast, so I brought the leftover tube in case we had to reapply later.

"You guys look spooky!" Soon-Yi came to greet us. Her clown costume was classic. She even had a spinning bow tie that glittered under the dance lights.

Maya had eight large, hairy legs that she controlled by a pull string. She showed us how she'd used bundles of gigantic straws for the leg segments and wrapped them with cheap black fuzz. They moved as if they were joined. Very realistic!

"I did a lot of research," she said with a wink before rushing over to greet Eddie.

There was a costume contest later, and I thought Eddie should win it. He was the best dog I'd ever seen. In fact, he looked a whole lot like the dog that had chased him.

Thanks to Tyler, everyone else, anyone who had fears, had used their costumes to conquer them!

Some of the students we talked to at lunch already had their costumes picked out, so we encouraged them to just add one thing to combat any fear they might have. Afraid of snakes? How about a cobra-themed bracelet? Afraid of water? Wear a life preserver! Scared of the dark? Bring a flashlight.

And they did. We convinced them all. We'd even managed to talk to the teachers who'd be chaperones. Facing fears became a theme for the night.

Tyler and I stood by the snack table admiring our work.

"High five," I told him, raising my hand.

"Adios, Scaremaster," Tyler replied, giving my hand a smack.

There was still the little matter of what it was that scared me, but I put that aside. At least for now, our classmates seemed safe.

There was a heaping platter of cookies next to the punch bowl. I reached for a celebratory cookie.

"Hang on," Tyler said, putting his hand into a hidden pocket at the back of his zombie shorts. He pulled out a handful of Dr. Rasmussen's pink vitamins. "Mom found these in our drawers."

He handed me one. "She said she was happy we felt better...." He imitated her voice. " '*But* if you don't take them, I'll come back to the party and pick you both up.' "

There was no laughing about it. We both knew she was serious.

He directed me to pour two cups of punch while he got out his phone.

"We have to prove we took them." Tyler laughed. "Stick out your zombie tongue." We were allowed to have phones at school parties so we could take pictures and call for rides and, in this case, show Mom we were healthy.

I did. He put a vitamin in my mouth and videotaped me swallowing.

I did the same for him, and then we both waved at the camera. "Thanks, Mom! Love ya!"

"Why'd she send so many?" I asked. Tyler had a whole bunch of those vitamins in his pocket.

"She didn't," Tyler said, as if that explained it. At my blank look, he continued, "She insisted I take a couple, but I didn't want to be typical Tyler the Turtle and end up being late, so I decided to do what Ryan the Rabbit would do. I grabbed the whole bottle and poured them into my pocket."

I laughed.

"Does Mom really think these cure everything on the planet and are harmless too?" I asked, noting what felt like a contradiction.

"That's what she said." Tyler then sent her the videos after titling them "The Cure-All."

Once that was done, we each ate a cookie, then went to dance.

The gym was completely transformed. Flashing lights and disco balls flickered at the center of the basketball court, where the dance floor had been set out. The hoops and bleachers were covered in black fabric. Carved pumpkins, fake gravestones, and plastic skeletons lined the edges of the room.

"Fantastic dog costume," I told Eddie, sliding up to him on the dance floor. I moved in slowly. If he was still mad at me, I could dance away.

He wasn't mad. In fact, he said, "Thanks for helping me with my fear. Dad's getting me a puppy!"

I smiled. This was the best Halloween ever. I rushed to Tyler and grabbed him in a bear hug.

"We rock, dude," I said happily.

"Uh, Ryan." Tyler pushed me back. "Notice anything strange?"

It was dark in the room, and the lights were flickering. The DJ was playing a song with a heavy beat.

"Why?"

"Well, I was dancing with Soon-Yi—"

"Wahoo!" I cut in.

"She's one of the few people here who can still tell us apart." He shook his head and went on. "We were having a good time, when suddenly, her eyes went blank. The pupils turned yellow. And she muttered something I couldn't understand before limping off the dance floor."

"Did she pull a muscle?" I asked.

"No. Look around." He turned me around so I could see her standing with some other kids by the cookie table.

Soon-Yi was wearing her clown costume, but now it was torn and dirty. Her arms appeared to be stiff by her sides. Her left leg dragged as she moved away from the refreshments and others filled that space. And she was making this strange sound that resonated across the gym. It was not quite a hum and not a growl but some odd combination of the two.

"I think she's a crawler," Tyler said so softly I made him repeat it.

"Nah," I said. "No way." As the words came out of my mouth, I started taking a closer look. A few kids from my history class were gathering near Soon-Yi.

One of them was now walking on all fours, like a cat, back arched and arms locked tight.

"Stalker," Tyler said. I could hear the panic rising in his voice.

Maya dropped to the ground and started dragging herself with her upper body.

"Another crawler."

The small group by the punch bowl was growing. Now there were two kids who looked a lot like me and Tyler. They bumped into each other as they struggled to stay upright when their muscles tore away.

"Boneys?" I asked, and he nodded. I tried to joke, "I think our costumes are better. We'd still win the contest for sure."

"Aren't you afraid?" Tyler asked. He shook my shoulders. "Our classmates are turning to zombies. Doesn't that scare you?"

I didn't know what to answer. I wasn't scared. I

was surprised, a little confused, and intensely curious, but not afraid.

"You gotta be scared of something." Tyler's eyes seemed to say: "Find something. Anything. Fast."

I wasn't scared. I shrugged. "What are they going to do? Eat our brains?"

"Maybe…" Tyler's eyes followed Eddie as he dashed past us at top speed. "Runner," he sighed. Those were the fast-moving zombies in the movies that were the first to attack. "It's just like the Scaremaster said. Everyone is turning into real zombies!"

In a flash, Tyler turned and faced me. "Think about it again, Ryan. Are you even a little afraid of our friends turning to zombies? 'Cause maybe if you are, you can stand up to your fear like the rest of us and that's how we defeat the Scaremaster." With everyone else facing their fears, it literally was just me who hadn't faced anything.

I tried to be scared. I really did. I closed my eyes and trembled. But it didn't work. I was energized and ready for whatever happened next, but no…I wasn't scared.

"I was doing some Internet research last night," Tyler told me while we backed into a corner where we could hide in the shadows while everyone we knew continued to transform. "Did you know there's a rare form of brain damage that keeps people from having any fears?"

"Are you saying I have brain damage?" If this was his attempt at a joke, my costume contest one was funnier.

"No...yes...Just that you might have damage to the amygdala." He went on. "Which could be why the Scaremaster can't affect you."

I considered what he was saying. Was there a medical reason I wasn't scared of anything? And if there was, could the Scaremaster's stories go on forever? That sounded terrifying...but still wasn't bad enough to shake me.

"Brain damage, eh? I prefer to think I am just really brave," I told Tyler.

"Uh, Ryan." Tyler grabbed my arm. "It's time to show me how brave you are."

He directed my attention to our zombie classmates, who had now formed a pack. They were moaning, crawling, limping, and dragging themselves toward us. They somehow sensed we weren't real zombies like them. (I bet the Scaremaster had put that into the story!) And that meant, if they were hungry, we'd make a delicious snack.

I should have been scared. Zombie apocalypse was a legitimate fear, so WHY WASN'T I SCARED? I wanted to be. Really I did!

I looked at the zombies and then at my brother. Sadly, I couldn't face my fears, but if we ever wanted to find a way to stop the Scaremaster, then survival was important. In humans versus zombies, the humans were outnumbered. There was only one thing to do.

"Tyler!" I shouted over the grunting, howling, humming din. "We gotta RUN!"

Chapter Nine

With the exception of Eddie the runner, zombies move slowly. That was the good news. The bad news was that we didn't know what they wanted and they just kept coming. More and more kids from the dance were turning into zombies, and they all had just one thing on their tiny, mutated brains: Get us.

Or more likely: Get Ryan. Of course, since we looked identical, the zombies couldn't tell who was who!

"I think they really do want to eat brains!" I told Tyler. The DJ was still playing loud dance music, so I shouted over my shoulder at the undead, "I have a malfunctioning amygdala! It'll taste terrible!"

That didn't stop them. We ran into the hallway, but they kept coming and coming.

Our school's classrooms each had two doors: one at the front by the chalkboard, and one farther down on the same wall, at the rear by the cabinetry. The rooms were all the same, with both doors leading into the same long, twisting hallway.

We rushed into a classroom by the main door and out the back door. The zombies, not smart enough to simply wait for us, followed. It was a parade of the moaning living dead, punctuated by the *swish-swish* of floppy body parts dragging against the industrial carpeting.

"Where do you think all the teachers are?" I asked Tyler as we bolted past the last classroom on the hallway, around the corner, and into the library. Inside, we ducked behind a tall bookshelf.

"I don't—" he started, when we both realized the moaning sounds had doubled.

A quick peek around the biographies answered my question. The teachers, staff, and dance chaperones were now all part of the zombie swarm.

"It's getting crowded in here!" I shouted over the constant hum of *gruhhhh*.

"This way." Tyler led me to a side door that I didn't know existed.

"How?" was all I asked.

"You don't come to the library much, do you?" he called out over the racket.

There was no reason to answer. We both knew it was true.

We made it back into the main hall and down to the lunchroom only to discover that there were a few zombies already there. It wasn't because they were smart and knew we'd be there eventually. No, these were the crawlers who had given up dragging their mutated bodies down the hallway after us. They were way too slow, so they'd just parked themselves in the cafeteria, where the food was stored.

The zombies had the large refrigerator open and were eating everything they could find. There were spilled bins of coleslaw, baked beans, and hot-dog packages all over the floor. The zombies had bitten through the coleslaw and bean containers and were eating the plastic wrappers with the hot dogs.

"Look," Tyler said. "If we can keep feeding them, they won't need to eat our brains."

"Your brain," I corrected, reminding him. "Mine's damaged."

"You're not giving that one up, are you?" He rolled his eyes. "Let's feed them!"

In the movies, crawler zombies were far scarier than they were in real life. In reality, they were my favorite! Even a slow, non-athletic person like me could outrun them. They moved like slugs, slithering along the floor without working limbs. The decayed teeth and yellow eyes were spooky, but I kept my face turned away as Tyler and I stepped over them, moving around the serving counter and into the school pantry.

"Oof," I said as I slipped on coleslaw juice.

Tyler grabbed my arm to stop me from taking a tumble.

"Thanks, man," I said, forever grateful.

Once in the pantry, I began opening a box of crackers.

"What are you doing?" Tyler asked, seeing me struggle with the wrapper. "Just throw the whole thing out there, and as far away from us as you can!"

I tossed out two boxes of crackers, which landed near the drinking fountain on the far wall. The zombies scampered toward them, diving over one another for the prize. The winners tore at the cardboard. The moaning increased. It was a cracker frenzy.

"We'll never have enough food for them all," I exclaimed, watching the stream of zombies now flooding in from the library. The entire school had been zombified.

Tyler checked out our food supply. "It looks like new deliveries come on Mondays. We have leftovers here, which isn't much."

"Gimme anything you got," I told him, warming up my throwing arm and wishing I was better at baseball.

"Uh, Ryan," Tyler said, pushing a box of dry noodles toward me, "we've got a problem."

I didn't like the sound of that. I shoved the noodles out toward Mr. Ramirez, who had just arrived on the scene, leading the zombie teachers' pack. "Wha—" I started, turning around. "You've got to be kidding me!"

Tyler was holding the Scaremaster's journal. "It was behind the noodles! But, Ry, I left it at home! I swear!"

"Figures." I grabbed the book and opened the first page. "That thing won't let us go."

How's it going, Ryan?
Scared yet?

We didn't have a pen, but there were some little mustard packets.

I tore one open and wrote **NO** with a yellow

finger. I wasn't going to give in, plus he'd know if I lied. We would defeat him some other way.

Let's make this scarier, then.

I sighed. I wish I knew *how* we were going to defeat him!

When I pulled away, I realized there were cookie crumbs stuck to my finger nail.

"Hey, Tyler," I started, but didn't have time to finish. The zombies, most likely thanks to the Scaremaster, had realized that the food was coming from the pantry. They didn't need me and Tyler to give it to them when it would be so much easier to serve themselves!

A hundred zombies made their move at once.

Okay, so I had to admit it, this was frightening. The way they marched or slithered forward as if they were all working together. But then again, I knew they weren't actually after me and Tyler—they just wanted the food—so I let whatever twinge of fear I might have felt pass over me.

We ducked under their outstretched arms and ran into the center of the room.

Tyler had the journal.

Rachel raised her head from the crowd of zombies and looked at me oddly. Her eyes didn't seem as yellow as the others', and yet she was moaning even louder than most. I turned away.

It was easier not to think of the zombies as our classmates and friends.

"Where do we go?" Tyler asked, voice high and tight. "Once they eat everything, they'll eat us." He knew a lot about zombies, so I trusted him. "After that, they'll spread into the neighborhood around school and break into houses to eat other people."

I'd seen a movie just like that. It was gruesome. Lots of blood and guts.

That should have scared me. But it didn't. "We need to stop them before they eat us, then."

I glanced back over my shoulder. We were still in the cafeteria, but the food was disappearing fast. "We can trap them inside," I suggested. "It'll buy us time."

"Time to do what?" Tyler was sounding pretty hopeless.

"Figure out how to stop the Scaremaster," I said. "And turn all our zombie friends and teachers back into normal friends and teachers."

We hustled out of the cafeteria and began

dragging desks and chairs from the closest class-room to block the doors. The doors were clear, and the zombies were pressing up against them, faces smashed against the glass. It looked like a zombie zoo. I hoped the doors wouldn't break.

"We need to keep feeding them until we figure out how to turn them back," I said, adding another chair to the furniture pile. The zombies rattled the doors. "Maybe there's more food in the teachers' lounge? And maybe, if we keep feeding them, they eventually get full, tired, and take a nap?"

"Zombies never get full!" Tyler shouted at me.

"Okay, calm down," I said, knowing he hated when I said that. "You're the logical one. If there's no food in the teachers' lounge, then..." I paused as my damaged brain began to spin. "There are cookies in the gym."

"And crumbs in the book," Tyler said, which inspired me to joke, "Let's feed the zombies the book!"

Hang on...it was so clear. Why hadn't I realized...

"Dude!" I gave my brother a fist bump. "He's using the cookies to turn everyone into zombies!"

"Of course!" Tyler said, feeling super excited to have part of this puzzle solved. "Everyone ate cookies!"

"There's a virus in the cookies." I hit my hand against the Scaremaster's journal. "Gotcha!"

Chapter Ten

We didn't know how to stop the virus, but at least we had a start. We'd discovered the source.

That was, until Tyler's full-amygdala brain kicked in. "We ate the cookies too," he reminded me.

Okay, so that added a wrinkle. "Maybe the Scaremaster wants to scare us so much, he gave us some kind of protection spell?"

"Does that make sense?" Tyler asked me. By his tone, it was clear he thought it didn't.

"Not really…" I didn't have time to come up with an alternative because, just then, Soon-Yi smashed her hand through the cafeteria's glass doors.

I could see Tyler was torn between wanting to help her and wanting to run away from her.

I made the decision for him.

"Run!" I shouted over the very loud zombie sounds that were now echoing in the hallway.

"Man, those dead dudes are noisy." My ears were starting to hurt.

More shattering glass came from our principal slamming his head through the door. The zombies had broken out.

Tyler and I only had two goals: Keep feeding them so they didn't eat us, then leave the building.

"Can we give them more cookies?" I shouted over the insane din. Fun fact: Movie zombies are never as noisy as the real thing.

"That's all we've got," Tyler said. "Cookies and..." He tapped his pocket, "Vitamins."

"I don't think those count as fooooooo..." My voice trailed off when Eddie, the fast-runner zombie-dog, grabbed my ankle. "Oof." He knocked me to the ground, then I was instantly dragged by a stalker zombie wearing a torn-up ninja costume and a vomiter, who promptly puked green gunk on my tennis shoe.

"Help!" I shouted to Tyler, who was now pretty far ahead of me. He didn't hear me. "Wait, Ty!" I didn't want to be zombie dinner!

Two crawlers crawled on top of me and pinned me down. I guess they weren't particular about whether the brains they ate were damaged because one of them, a hippie zombie, opened her mouth to reveal the sharpest fangs I'd ever seen.

I had a feeling flood through me that was completely unfamiliar. Was this fear? All I could do was stare at her sharp incisors as the feeling became more and more pronounced. It wasn't that she was a zombie...it was those nasty, pointed teeth. She leaned in toward my neck.

I began to tremble. It was overwhelming, and for a moment, I didn't know what to do.

In a panicked move, I shoved back at her with all my might, managing to break away for a second before her friend, a ballerina crawler, pounced and pulled me back down to the hard floor.

Now they both snarled at me with those same pointed teeth...decayed, brown, sharp, glistening with blood.

I shut my eyes against them and shrieked, "TYLER!"

I thought I was a goner, when suddenly I was showered with something crumbly. And sweet-smelling.

The zombies got off me and moved aside just enough that I could scramble to my feet.

"Cookies!" Tyler announced, standing there

with a giant smile. He was tossing them in the air like confetti. "Delicious cookies! Come and get them!"

The massive tray was about half empty from the dance, but there were still quite a few left.

"Thanks," I told Tyler, because what else is there to say to the guy who saved your life?

"You're welcome," he answered, tossing more cookies in the air.

"What are we going to do when they're gone?" I moved closer to him. My heartbeat was finally settling back to normal.

He gave me a shrug. "There's punch in the punch bowl?" Tyler was now sprinkling cookies around the zombies as if he was feeding barnyard chickens.

"Do zombies even get thirsty?"

That was beyond his zombie knowledge. And I'd never seen movie zombies stop for refreshments. Tyler shrugged again.

As he was getting close to the bottom of the tray, I started to worry. "We can open lockers to see if anyone forgot their lunch," I suggested. "And we still haven't checked the teachers' lounge.

I know they have coffee.... Maybe there are stale donuts?"

"It won't be enough," Tyler said. Some of the zombies weren't finding whole cookies anymore, and battles were breaking out over the few that remained. "Another problem: We only have about an hour before parents come for pickup!"

I couldn't even wrap my head around Mom walking in on this supernatural disaster.

Tyler and I were gradually being backed into a corner as the zombies crept toward us, looking for more to eat.

The tray was now empty.

"I guess we're going to become one of the pack," I said, feeling like this was the end. "Think Mom will be mad if her kids are zombies?"

"I'm sure she'll immediately ask Dr. Rasmussen to invent a cure." Tyler said, and in that moment, we both turned to each other and shouted in twin time, "That's it!"

To get away from the zombies gathered around our feet, Tyler threw the silver cookie tray. It made a loud clatter at the end of the hall, and some of the zombies headed toward it to see if there were any more crumbs. Others stayed put, but it was enough of a distraction that we managed to break away and fly to the gym like our feet were on fire.

It was depressing. All the decorations had been torn down. The lights still glowed and the music played, but no one was dancing. The DJ must have eaten cookies too, because he'd come in a suit and now looked like he'd risen from the dead. Still, he manned his post at the turntable and continued to announce the next song in slurred *uuh*s.

Tyler and I got to the punch bowl before anyone, even Eddie. He'd gone after the clattering tray, which bought us a few minutes before his inevitable realization that we'd gone.

There were ten of Dr. Rasmussen's Cure-All vitamins in Tyler's pocket. He crumbled them up and dropped the entire collection into the punch bowl with a splash and started stirring with the ladle.

"We ate the cookies but didn't get the virus," he said, voicing what we'd both figured out.

"I'm guessing Dr. Rasmussen doesn't know that his cure includes the zombie virus," I said. "If this works, we should tell him."

"It's an untouched market," Tyler said. "He'd make millions."

There was a crazy-loud clang as the zombies began entering the gym. The moaning and the music and the scrape of dragging legs filled the room.

Assuming our new drink concoction worked to cure the virus, we only had one last problem to solve. How were we going to get the zombies to drink it?

Chapter Eleven

"We have to search for donuts," I told Tyler. "It's our only hope."

"There's no time," he replied. The zombies were surrounding us.

"Sacrifice yourself?" I suggested, but after seeing the horrified look on his face, then said, "Just kidding."

I actually had a plan.

"Remember how we were going to switch places at the dance?" I touched my new short haircut. "No time like now."

Tyler didn't have time to consider it.

He stayed at the punch bowl, shouting, "Fresh, delicious brains," while I ran to the entrance of the gym. I was counting on the fact that zombies couldn't think clearly. And that they couldn't process that there were two of us, even though most of them knew us personally, plus having just seen us together moments ago in the library and cafeteria!

When they got close to Tyler, I whistled the family whistle and shouted, "Hey, lame brains!"

It wasn't enough. They were still gathering around Tyler. I saw the two girls with the sharp teeth working their way to the front of the crowd.

I was going to need something louder to attract their attention. I hurried to the DJ stage and grabbed his microphone. "Follow me!" I shouted through the speakers, then whistled again. The zombies—all of them—turned toward me, and when I bolted to the door, they took off after me.

I made it as far as the lockers before I needed help.

How did Eddie get to be a runner? That was my first thought as he knocked me down again. He wasn't usually athletic! My second thought was to be grateful that he was the only fast one. I'd have lost my brains long ago otherwise.

I fell to the ground and scrambled to get up before the other zombies reached me. One ankle biter nearly had my toes when Tyler appeared by the library doors.

"Hey, creeps! You can't catch me." He whistled,

then slammed his hands against the library doors, making a racket before dashing off.

We had to swap places one more time before I made it to the teachers' lounge. I was concerned about leaving my brother in the hallway with a hundred hungry zombies, but he waved me off.

"Go!" Tyler shouted. Then, having learned from our previous experience, he started ducking in and out of classrooms in a serpentine fashion. The zombies followed him into the front classroom doors and out the back. It would have been funny, if it wasn't so dangerous!

"Protect your fancy brains!" I shouted at Tyler as I opened the lounge door.

Coffee. Creamer.

A pink box! I was so happy I could sing. Then I opened the lid.

There was one crummy donut left. And it was the gross kind with coconut topping.

This was a real-life nightmare.

I started tossing school supplies, teaching manuals, and paper plates onto the floor as I went from cabinet to cabinet, hoping to find something edible.

I was ready to feed the zombies a kindergarten diet of construction paper and paste when I found what I needed behind a stack of mugs. Two big bags of potato chips. The bags were a little dusty, but the chips would soak up the punch and I didn't think the zombies would care if they were expired. If they'd eat brains, who'd complain about stale potato chips?

I took the bags, then told Tyler to reverse course back to the gym.

He got to the snack table first, while I had to fight off Mr. Ramirez, who had grabbed my waist. With my free hand, I tossed Tyler the bags. He opened them and dumped the chips into the punch bowl.

Tyler was grabbing soggy potato chips by the handful out of the punch bowl and throwing them at the zombies when Mr. Ramirez suddenly let go and dove for Tyler instead. It was in that moment I remembered the guy was also the basketball coach. He was fast and fit.

Tyler went down with a crash and a loud "ouch."

But worse than the fact that he'd have a bruise on his butt was that the coach knocked over the table. The punch bowl teetered, as if in slow motion, then slammed to the floor, spilling punch-soaked potato chips everywhere.

Every zombie in the school went crazy. They were slipping in punch, stepping on chips, sliding all over each other, and growling with bared teeth as they put their faces to the floor and lapped up the last remaining food in the building.

Tyler managed to get up, holding his butt. He carefully stepped over the zombies, walking through chip gunk, and made his way to me. "If this doesn't work, we're doomed."

There was no way that either of us was going into that undead slippery pile to make sure everyone got a treat.

So we stood by the side, as far out of the way as we could, and hoped that no parents arrived early for pickup.

"Should we leave?" I asked. "Save ourselves?"

As long as the zombies were having a juicy potato-chip picnic, we could make a dash for the door.

"Common sense says yes," Tyler answered. I knew what that meant. Curiosity meant we should stay.

We stayed.

We wanted to know what would happen. Besides, if the cure-all didn't work, we'd be zombified anyway. We'd never get far enough away that Eddie couldn't catch us and drag us back again.

Soon-Yi was the first one to stand up from the zombie pile. She rose, licking her lips, which were pink from the punch. In the light from the disco ball, I could see her eyes tracing the room.

"I think she's looking for us," Tyler said, pulling me back into the shadows.

"I think she's looking for you," I replied, and then spontaneously shoved him into the light.

Her eyes immediately caught his.

"Oh, that was a bad move," I said, trying to drag him back. "I think maybe we should make a run for it. It's our only chance!"

"No." Tyler pulled his arm out of my grip. "It's working, Ryan. The cure is working."

Soon-Yi still looked like a zombie to me.

"She recognizes me," Tyler explained. "She's not brain-dead anymore. She knows who I am!" He was more excited than I'd seen him since the day she'd first asked what page we were on.

Gradually, other kids stood up from the floor. Maya glanced around, looking confused. I heard her ask Rachel, "Is this a new dance?"

Rachel gave me a hard stare from across the room. I couldn't wait to hear what tales she'd tell on Monday.

It wasn't just that people were getting their heads back together, but the yellow in their eyes was fading, their arms were working, their legs stopped dragging, their fangs disappeared, and the costumes that had gone all zombie were back to being clean, pristine, and looking as if the last two hours had never happened.

"Ryan, look!" Tyler drew my attention to the DJ, who was wandering around by the stage. He was still a zombie!

"We need to get the cure to him, or he might spread the virus all over again," I said, but it looked like the chips were gone and there was no way we'd get him to lick the floor to get a last drop of punch.

"Maya!" Tyler rushed over to her and asked if he could have a part of her spider arm. She didn't understand, but he promised to give it back.

The zombie DJ began to wander through the room. He hadn't eaten all night, and I wondered whose brains he would pick first. If the Scaremaster were still telling the story, it would most definitely be mine.

Tyler handed me one of the straws that made up Maya's spider arms.

I scraped potato goo from the bottom of Tyler's shoe and make a spitball from it.

"You have to have perfect aim," Tyler warned me. "One chance."

I took a deep breath. I had to wait until the zombie came toward me, his mouth wide open. I could smell his rotten breath.

"Are you scared?" Tyler asked. "Maybe this is what we've been expecting all night?"

"I...no...I..." I pushed away a small thought that was forming at the back of my head and lifted Maya's straw arm to my mouth.

"Face your fear!" Tyler shouted at me.

I let the zombie get a few steps closer. When he bared his decayed teeth, I shot the spitball into his mouth.

He swallowed hard.

It wasn't clear at first whether it had worked, but then the DJ suddenly backed away from me and, just like that, he was back at the turntable.

The teachers wandered the edges of the room, back to being the chaperones.

Everyone paired up to dance.

There were no more snacks and the floor was

sticky with punch, but no one cared. The DJ changed tunes, and as the music got louder and faster, everyone began to rock out.

"We beat the Scaremaster!" I cheered.

"Was it the last zombie that did it?" Tyler asked, but then answered his own question with a laugh, "A hundred zombies attacked, and it turned out you were afraid of the DJ!"

I didn't laugh because back in the hallway, and again facing the DJ, I'd realized there was something else. The Scaremaster had indeed uncovered my biggest fear. I just didn't know if he knew what he'd done.

I shook off my suspicions.

Now wasn't the time to think about what the Scaremaster had or hadn't done. I didn't want to think at all.

Now it was time to dance!

Tyler and I jumped into the middle of the dance floor, not worried this time that we'd be tackled.

We danced for a few songs and then noticed that it was almost time for the party to end. The teachers had forgotten about the costume contest, which was fine. Everyone who had faced a fear that night deserved the prize.

I pulled Tyler to the side. We had a few things to do before Mom showed up.

I was pretty sure that Mrs. Clancy would find out about the mess in the cafeteria and the hall, and had no doubt that somehow Tyler and I would get blamed.

"I'm not afraid of detention," Tyler told me.

"It's not so bad," I said. "We can pass notes."

"But no telling stories." Tyler gave me a small smile.

"No stories," I agreed.

Tyler had stashed the Scaremaster's journal behind the DJ station when he'd first come back to the gym to get the cookies. He went to get it.

Rachel stopped him on the way back across the room. I rushed over there to find out what she was saying. The last thing we needed was her reminding everyone that there'd nearly been a zombie apocalypse at school.

"So," she said as Tyler tried to hide the book under his shirt, "is that really the Scaremaster's journal?"

"Huh?" Tyler and I looked at each other. I knew what he'd say later—it was statistically impossible that we hadn't just heard the same thing.

"My cousin went to summer camp. She came home talking about a book whose stories came true," Rachel said. "It's just a rumor, though. No way what she said actually happened." Rachel pointed at the book, which was a big square lump under Tyler's shirt. "I hate rumors," she said. "Don't you?" Rachel raised an eyebrow. "By the way, I'm allergic to chocolate." She winked and walked away.

"Does that mean she didn't eat the cookies?" Tyler asked me.

"She's smart! She stayed safe by pretending to be a zombie," I said, adding with a laugh, "I'm starting to really like her."

We were dressed like zombies, but we'd never actually acted like them. From the moment we had realized what was going on, we'd run. I wondered what would have happened if we'd joined the moaning pack instead.

It also crossed my mind to wonder whether there were other kids who'd faked their transition.

Who else might have avoided the cookies? Was anyone allergic to other ingredients? I had a vibe that Eddie might have avoided gluten, but I couldn't remember for sure. Hmmm. Very interesting...

Rachel didn't get too far before she turned back. "Be sure to hide that book where no one will ever find it." Then she disappeared into the dancing crowd.

"I know just the place," Tyler said.

We hurried to the library. He found a spot on a far-back shelf on the very top row, in between boring-looking books about Transylvanian history.

"I'd never look there," I told him. Before he boosted me up so I could slip the book in the slot, we used the leftover fake blood I'd brought to smear across the pages. We couldn't destroy it, so I wanted to mess up the book as much as possible, making it so that no one else would want it if they found it. I put blood smears on every page until the tube was empty and the book was ruined.

Then we stashed it on the bookshelf, where it hopefully would stay for infinity.

After that, we didn't spend any more time thinking about the book or the Scaremaster. Our friends were in the gym, and we didn't want to miss the party. It was an epic Halloween!

"Last dance," the DJ called.

"Meet you after," Tyler told me, before hurrying off.

"Where are you going?" I asked.

"The Scaremaster ruined my first dance," he called over his shoulder. "I'm not going to let that happen again."

Next thing I knew, he was swaying to the beat with Soon-Yi.

I stood by the edge of the dance floor, alone, watching our friends and teachers. It was over. The Scaremaster had had his fun, and now it was done. I leaned back against the wall and wondered if things had started to shift once I'd discovered my own fear, or if that was just coincidence.

It was the teeth that made me realize what scared me most. And now that I was thinking about it, it seemed unusual for two zombies to have such large, protruding fangs. The way they'd moved in toward me made my heart race. I had been afraid they'd bite my neck. Suck my blood. Turn me into one of them.

I'd seen hundreds of vampire movies, but none of them had made me feel this terrified.

Turned out the Scaremaster had done exactly what he'd said he was going to do. He'd discovered my greatest fear.

My greatest fear was vampires.

Epilogue

"The ski slopes look amazing," Zoe exclaimed. She was standing with her best friend Matt in front of the large glass window next to his sofa bed. The rental cabin was small, but had just enough space for both the Ortiz and Lancaster families to be together. Twelve-year-old Zoe would have to share a room with her eight-year-old sister, Chloe, while Matt slept on the pull-out couch in the living room.

"Yeah. Amazing," Matt agreed. There was nothing blocking the view between the cabin and the steep face of the mountain. He pushed back his slick light brown hair and stared out, as if planning his first run of the day.

"Hey, Lancaster, check it out." Matt put his hand on Zoe's shoulder and pointed to the bottom of the slopes.

Matt was twelve, like Zoe, but because he was tall,

everyone thought he was older. He pointed past the ski lift, toward a shadowed building across the road. Zoe rose on her tiptoes to see what he'd discovered.

"That's the old lodge I read about online," Matt said. "It's supposed to be haunted."

"Oh, cool!" Zoe squinted through the window, pressing her nose against the cold glass for a better look.

The old lodge was three stories high, but it was partially blocked by modern buildings. Zoe could see the pointed tips of tall, imposing spires, like on a castle. Now that she knew where to look, she pushed past Matt to a small side window in the kitchen where she could get an even better view.

Part of the roof appeared to have crumbled from the weight of several sharp icicles that hung off the side of the building. They looked like a row of deadly tiger fangs.

Along the front of the place, dark gray paint was peeling, and the steep porch was completely caved in on one side.

Zoe squinted at the house, staring at a dark spot in an upper window, when suddenly, the shadow moved. "Whoa, what was—" she started.

"Did you see that?!" Matt poked his finger at the living room window. It left a steamy print.

"I don't know," Zoe said cautiously. "Maybe. But it could have just been the sunset reflecting on the lodge's shattered glass."

"We gotta check it out," Matt said.

"Great," Zoe told him. It was getting dark. If they were going to go to the old lodge, it had to be right away.

Zoe went into the bedroom to ask her parents for permission to explore. Everyone said she looked like her mother, with peach skin, straight light hair, and green eyes, while Chloe had darker skin and thick brown hair like their dad.

"Can I go with Matt to check out the lodge?" Zoe asked. She intentionally left which "lodge" vague. If they got in trouble later, she could always play it off like, "Oh, you thought I meant the *new* lodge?" Zoe would then nod and reply, "That's funny because I meant the old one." And they'd all have a good laugh.

At least in Zoe's imagination that was how it would happen.

Her mom studied Zoe's face for a long moment, then said, "Meet us in the dining room for dinner."

Then she added, "We're talking about the new lodge, right?"

Zoe's mom was a mind reader. There was no other possibility. That was why she always seemed to know what Zoe was thinking. Zoe's mom had an uncanny ability to stop her plans before anything bad—or interesting—could happen.

"Of course," Zoe said, giving in to the fact that exploring the old lodge would have to wait.

Zoe looked at the time on her cell phone. "Dinner. Got it." Then she noticed the phone had no service. "I wonder if the lodge has Wi-Fi," she muttered to herself as she went to meet up with Matt, who'd been having a similar conversation with his parents.

"They don't want us to stray from the lodge," Matt said as they hurried outside into the bitter cold. "Dad said 'new lodge,' like he knew where we really wanted to go."

"Same." Zoe's coat kept most of her warm, but her nose was frozen. She stuffed her gloved hands into her jacket with a mental note to take a scarf when they went skiing. "It's okay." She pinched her lips together and said, "We should do some research on that old place before we investigate, anyway."

They walked around a little while, then went into the main reception area. Matt flopped down into a very soft leather couch in front of a large wood-burning fire. The overstuffed pillows made a windy, gassy sound. He laughed while Zoe sat down gently, rolling her eyes at him.

"I hope the slopes are awesome because this place is kind of boring," Matt said, resting his head back against the fluffy cushions.

"You think the Wampir Lodge is boring?" a woman sitting nearby repeated his words. She leaned around the high wings of a small velvet chair. Zoe hadn't noticed her when they came in.

The lady seemed out of place in her glamorous, high-necked, old-fashioned gown and small, veiled hat. She was thin, with long hair and brown eyes, No, yellow eyes. No, they were definitely green. They looked like they kept changing.

"Come with me," the woman said, rising. "I'd like to show you something special."

"Uh," Zoe stalled. She didn't think going off with a stranger was a smart idea.

"Have you seen the lodge's library?" the woman asked, moving in closer to Zoe and Matt.

"Library?" Matt asked. "There's a library?" He hadn't seen one on the resort map.

"Certainly you've noticed that there is no phone service at the lodge," she said, looking at Zoe with eyes that were now violet.

"We noticed," Matt said with a groan.

The woman nodded sympathetically. "It's quiet here at night."

"We're gonna want something to do after skiing, snowboarding, campfires, and carriage rides," Zoe told Matt with a shrug. "Looks like we're going to need some books."

Matt considered the problem. "I guess, if there are some scary stories...." He was clearly trying to wrap his head around this Internet disaster. "That could pass the time."

"Follow me," the woman told them. "I'm certain you will find exactly what you need."

Since they weren't leaving the lodge, Zoe figured it was okay to go with her.

The library was a small room off the main lobby. There were two plush reading chairs, a small desk with pens and paper, and a tall shelf of books.

At the top of the shelf was a sign.

It read:

Give One/Take One

"What does that mean?" Zoe asked the woman, wondering if she worked at the lodge.

Pointing a long, bony finger at the sign, the woman explained, "If you brought a book from home, you can leave it here once you've finished and take a new one."

"I didn't bring anything," Zoe said, wishing she had. She'd been reading a soccer biography about one of her favorite players but didn't pack it.

"I didn't bring anything either," Matt said. "I thought I'd be using my laptop to watch TV."

The woman's eyes shifted to black as she said, "Don't worry. Just take whichever book you want. When you reach the end of the story, you can put it back here before you leave for home."

"Okay," Matt said as he and Zoe began to look through the shelves, starting at the very top and going down row by row. There were romance novels, cowboy novels, and a lot of mysteries. But no scary stories.

"This stinks," Matt declared after reaching the bottom shelf. "There's nothing to read!"

"I don't think you've looked hard enough,"

the woman said, silently approaching from behind them. She reached up to the top shelf, in the middle of the row, and pulled out a strange-looking book.

Zoe swore she'd looked past that spot. How had she missed that book? It was clearly the most interesting one in the library.

The book was an antique leather-bound journal with a small brass clasp. The most fascinating part was that the cover had several strange triangles etched into the leather. They seemed to have been painted gold at some point, but the color had faded with age.

The woman handed the book to Matt. As it passed by Zoe, she thought she smelled a sharp metallic odor rising from the leather. Matt opened the book and set it on the small desk so they could both look inside. The pages were made of a thick, yellowed paper, slightly tinged brown around the edges.

On the first page were the words:

Tales from the Scaremaster

But beneath that title, the rest of the page was blank.

Zoe flipped a few pages. "They're all blank."

"Since you like scary stories," the woman advised, "perhaps you could write your own tales?" Over her shoulder there was a small window that looked out toward the old, run-down Wampir Lodge. "There must be something around here that would inspire you," she hinted, glancing back at Zoe and Matt.

She handed Zoe a pen from the desk. "You could start now," the woman said, her voice low and even. It was a bit hypnotic, like a magician Zoe had once seen at a fair.

There was something inside Zoe that felt like the woman wasn't going to let them leave the library until they'd written something. Not like she was locking them in, but rather, she wanted them to write so badly that she'd stay with them until they did.

Matt told Zoe, "You start the story and I'll jump in when I have an idea."

"Okay," she agreed. Not wanting to let the woman down, since she was the one who had discovered the journal, Zoe wrote, "Once upon a time, Matteo Ortiz and Zoe Lancaster were looking for adventure at the Wampir Ski Resort and Lodge."

"Wait!" Matt suddenly pointed at the page. "Look!"

Under Zoe's writing, there were new words. She hadn't written them. And neither had Matt.

Looking for a scare, are you? The Scaremaster won't disappoint you. You shouldn't have started this story. Now I get to finish it!

Read Zoe and Matt's story
(if you dare) in

TALES FROM THE
SCAREMASTER™

VAMPIRE
VACATION

SCHOOL OF FEAR

Sharpen your pencils and put on a brave face.
The School of Fear is waiting for YOU!
Will you banish your fears and graduate on time?

IT'S NEVER TOO LATE TO APPLY!

www.EnrollinSchoolofFear.com